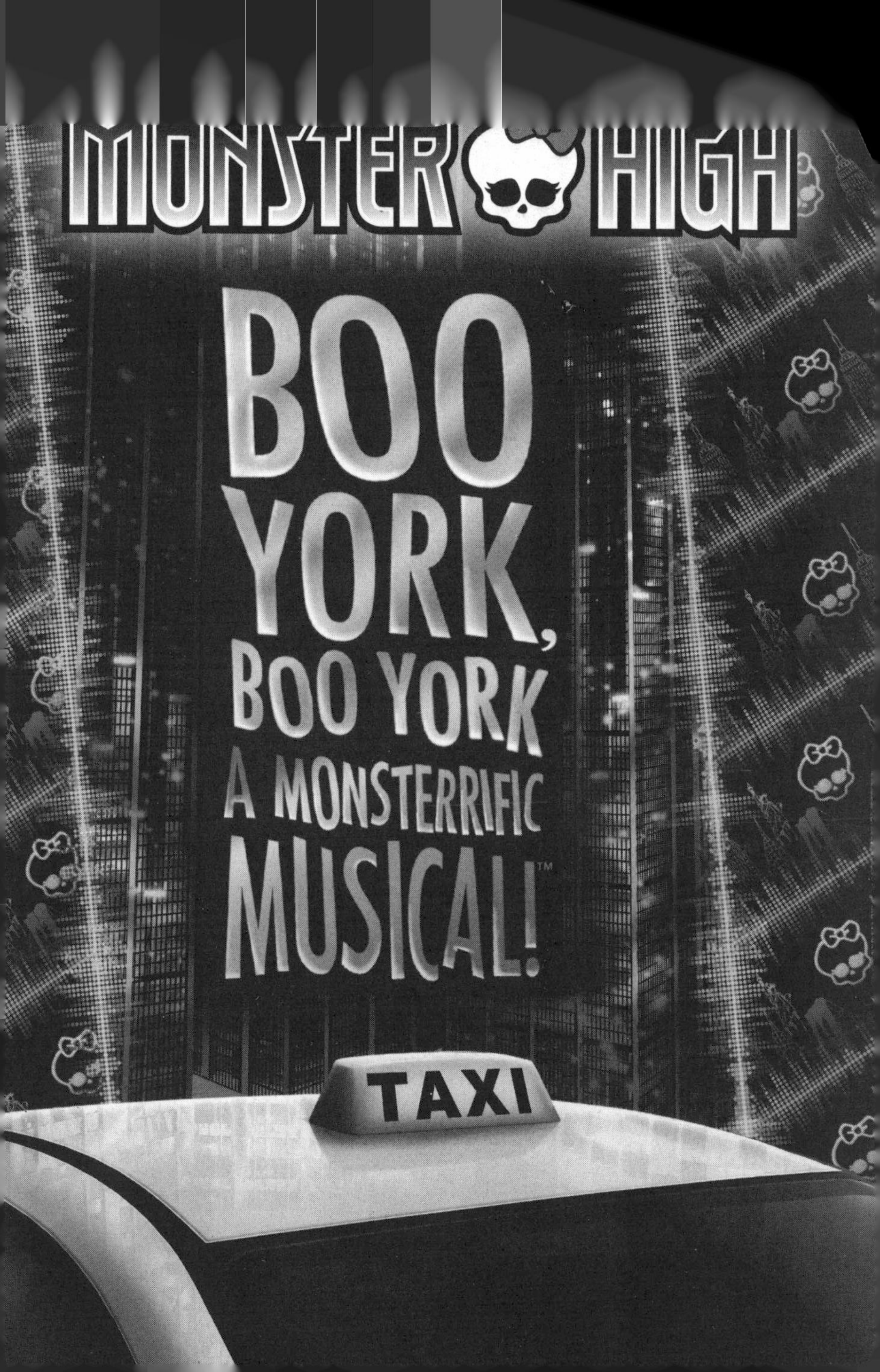
MONSTER HIGH
BOO YORK, BOO YORK
A MONSTERRIFIC MUSICAL!™
TAXI

Little, Brown and Company

Hachette Book Group
1290 Avenue of the Americas, New York, NY 10104
Visit us at lb-kids.com

Little, Brown and Company is a division of Hachette Book Group, Inc.
The Little, Brown name and logo are trademarks of Hachette Book Group, Inc.

The publisher is not responsible for websites (or their content) that are not owned by the publisher.

First Edition: September 2015

ISBN 978-0-316-30119-0

10 9 8 7 6 5 4 3

RRD-C

Printed in the United States of America

# MONSTER HIGH

# BOO YORK, BOO YORK
## A MONSTERRIFIC MUSICAL!™

### The Junior Novel

ADAPTED BY
**Perdita Finn**

BASED ON THE SCREENPLAY BY
**Keith Wagner**

Ⓛ Ⓑ

LITTLE, BROWN AND COMPANY
New York   Boston

# CHAPTER 1

## The Purr-fect Pop Star

The skyline of Boo York shone in the darkness. Lights blazed from the Monster of Liberty's torch, the top of the Vampire State Building, the golden Ptolemy Tower, and the flashing neon signs of Times Scare. But the brightest light of all was a fiery comet shooting across the sky.

From inside a packed theater on Bloodway, a spotlight revealed Catty Noir opening her mouth onstage to sing her hit ballad, "Love Is a Storm." The crowd cheered. Cameras clicked. The stage lit up with pyrotechnic fires, illuminating a backdrop of diamond-like pieces of broken mirrors. Catty's pink mane of hair, the same color as her sequined gown, fell to her waist in long, soft curls. Her dark eyes were full of soul. Pure, pitch-perfect notes filled the arena of Madison Scare Garden. No wonder Catty Noir was an international pop sensation and *Thrillboard* magazine's musician of the century. She could sing about love like no other monster.

"*Love is like a storm tonight. Love in the air, love in the clouds, love like a flood!*"

As her voice hit the last note, the crowd began to clap and cheer. Catty bowed and blew kisses to the audience. "Thank you! I love you, Boo York! Good-bye!" After the curtain came down, Catty slipped out of the back of the theater and headed to her waiting limo. Black-suited security gargoyles kept back the crowds as fans thrust programs and autograph books toward her to sign. Catty tried to smile, but she was overwhelmed by the glare of her success. As the door shut behind her, Catty closed her eyes. She was exhausted.

The next day, *Thrillboard* magazine's cover story was about Catty. But it wasn't about the concert—the big news was that Catty, the queen of the love song, was dropping out of show business! But why? No one knew…except Catty.

# CHAPTER 2

# What a Ghoul Wants

The bell rang, and monsters grabbed their homework and slammed their lockers shut. It was another busy day at Monster High. Catty grabbed her backpack and smiled at Frankie Stein and Draculaura. Frankie, a voltageous mint-green ghoul who was brought to life in her dad's laboratory, and Draculaura, the vegetarian vampire daughter of Dracula, were friends of Catty's. They had taken such good care of her ever since she had dropped out of the music scene to come and be an ordinary ghoul again.

"Well, I'm off to the rehearsal room!" Catty announced.

Frankie smiled. "Can't wait to hear your next

song!" She still couldn't believe that a pop sensation had become one of her dearest friends.

"Good luck with the music-writey stuff!" Draculaura exclaimed.

As Catty strolled down the hallway, monsters called out greetings to her. She was one of them now, and so she had something to write about other than stage lights and limousines. She knew what it was like to be a real ghoul again. If only she could find the right words to express everything that was in her heart.

She flicked on the light above the stage and sat down at the piano. "Finally, I can write a song for me. About something that really matters. Something that I know. Something I have lived," she whispered to herself.

She tried out some chords, scribbled them down on music sheets, stared at them, and then crumpled the sheets up. Soon, the floor around her was covered in paper. Frankie and Clawdeen Wolf walked by, peeked into the auditorium, and saw Catty slam her fists into the keyboard in frustration.

Clawdeen, fierce fashionista, daughter of the Werewolf, and Frankie's other BMFF, giggled. "Genius at work!"

But Catty didn't feel like a genius. The problem was that she wanted to write a love song, a great love song, but she didn't know anything about love. Not really. She sighed. "I've never had that music in my heart." Alone, she could admit the truth. "I feel like a fake. I have to find my own voice! My own music!"

She got up from the piano, frustrated, and began climbing a spiral staircase that led to the roof of the school. She wanted to know what love felt like, and she wanted to sing about it in her own voice. But would she ever find true love?

She passed a room where couples were listening to music and dancing. "*I try and try but I can't catch hold; there's a fire that burns inside me,*" she sang.

She came onto the roof and saw the sky twinkling with stars. She felt full of emotion, as if some secret were hidden for her there. "*Oh, now I've seen what I've tried to find. I've been looking far and wide. High and low, low and high. In the dark, now I've found the light.*" The words were pouring out of her.

Catty leaned against a wall. Carved into it were a heart and initials, symbols of a love she still didn't know.

Just then something close to the horizon caught her eye. It was the faint light of a shimmering comet.

It flared and pulsed with a blue aura. The beauty of it made Catty gasp. She leaned over the railing and reached her hands out toward it.

"I guess I've been looking in the wrong place the entire time," Catty realized. "Maybe I should search inside."

# CHAPTER  3

## Bad Hair Day

The glow of the comet was reflected in the De Niles' fancy swimming pool. Ramses de Nile, father of Egyptian princesses Cleo and Nefera, was peering through a telescope up at the sky.

"The long wait has come to its end," he said out loud, pleased. "After thirteen hundred years, it is time." With a swirl of his magnificent white robes, he swept past tall pillars rimmed with hieroglyphics and a magnificent peacock throne and marched back into his palatial mansion.

Cleo's older sister, Nefera, was curled up in a chair reading when he came in.

"Nefera, my daughter," commanded Ramses, "summon your sister, Cleo, and pack your bags. We travel to meet our dynastic destiny to Boo York City."

Nefera was thrilled at the thought of a trip. "Boo York City! Clawesome!" she shrieked, but then she realized her younger sister was coming too. "Does Cleo have to come?" she whined.

"Nefera de Nile!" Ramses scolded her. Having two Egyptian princesses in one palace could be a lot of work sometimes.

Cleo was thrilled about the upcoming trip. It was all she could talk about the next day in school. She downloaded all her favorite photos of the city's hot spots and kept pulling out her iCoffin to show everyone where she was headed. "That's right. I'm going to Boo York City!" she kept explaining. "I'm so excited I'm about to burst through my bandages."

Walking through the hallway of Monster High, her arm linked through Deuce's, she kept flipping through the images without looking up. Kids jumped out of her way to avoid collisions, and she didn't even notice.

Deuce Gorgon, Cleo's boyfriend, was happy for her, and he grinned. "Sounds pretty sweet, Cleo. What's the occasion?"

"Daddy's taking us to a very exclusive gala opening at the Boo York Museum of Unnatural History," she gushed.

Deuce scratched one of the snakes on his head. "Uh, okay, cool?"

Cleo couldn't believe he didn't know what she was talking about! "Oh, Deuce," she sighed. "It's the first public showing of the most important Egyptian artifact ever—the comet crystal!"

The bell rang, and Cleo was still talking nonstop about the big event when they settled into their desks in the classroom. She handed Deuce her iCoffin, which now displayed a picture of the famous comet crystal. "It's a little stone that fell from the comet thirty-nine hundred years ago, three thingies, you know, when it circles around?"

Ghoulia Yelps, who was sitting behind Deuce, leaned forward to check out the crystal. She moaned.

Cleo nodded her head at her brainy zombie ghoulfriend. "Okay, circumgyrations. Whatevs. When the pyramids were young. They say the crystal gains magical powers when the original comet passes overhead!"

"Uh. . ." Deuce gulped, still not sure what to say. "Okay, cool?"

That afternoon at the Casketball game, Cleo was still talking about Boo York while she sat next to Deuce on the bleachers. Clawd Wolf, Clawdeen's brother, was on the court dribbling the ball and being pursued by a giant Cyclops.

"Go, Clawd!" shouted Draculaura.

Cleo did not appreciate being interrupted. "Anyway, so the original comet is on its way back toward Earth, so they're finally unveiling the comet crystal."

The ref blew his whistle just as Clawd dropped the Casketball through the hoop. The crowd cheered, except for Cleo, who was too preoccupied with her thoughts of Boo York.

"You haven't heard the best part," she confided to her boyfriend as they headed to their lockers after the game was over. "You are coming with me, Deuce!"

Deuce stopped in his tracks and gulped again. He couldn't believe it. "For reals?"

Cleo tossed her highlighted hair. Her gold jewelry jangled. "Oh. My. Ra! You are going to love it! We get to go to his big fancy gala at the museum, get all dressed up, rub wrapped elbows with all of the Egyptian dignitaries!" She grinned happily at the thought.

Deuce tried to hide how uneasy he felt. He adjusted the sunglasses he always wore so he wouldn't turn his fellow monsters into stone. "I don't really do big and fancy," he said.

"Oh, Deuce!" Cleo giggled, touching him affectionately on the arm as if he were joking with her. "And at midnight we all go up on the roof of the museum and watch the great comet shoot across the sky! I want you looking clawesome." She swiped off his sunglasses, and Deuce quickly shut his eyes. Cleo pulled out a pair of designer shades and slipped them on his face. "Booci sunglasses," she said.

Deuce grinned. "All right!"

"And," said Cleo, clapping her hands delightedly, "I got this for you to wear in Boo York!" She opened up her locker and pulled out a beard made of solid gold, just like the best mummies in Egypt wore, with a braid down the center.

Deuce cocked a single eyebrow, uncertain. Cool shades were one thing. A heavy fake beard was another. "All...right?" he said tentatively.

Cleo held it up to Deuce's face and stuck it on to his chin. All the twisting green snakes of Deuce's gorgon hair began to hiss. "Oh, Deucy! You look so high class! We're going to one of the most fashionable cities in the world, and I want my manster looking freaky fabulous!"

The snakes were hissing and trying to reach down and pull off the beard.

Cleo felt a moment of worry but shrugged it off. "Here," she said. "I'll just hang on to this for you until we get to Boo York." She pulled the beard off Deuce's chin and tucked it back into her backpack.

Deuce rubbed his face. "I don't know, Cleo. Dressing up, fancy galas, solid gold Egyptian beardy things. I don't know anything about that rich people stuff. I mean, your dad already doesn't think I'm good enough for you. What if we get there and I embarrass you?"

Cleo took Deuce's hand and smiled. "You? Embarrass me?" she said sincerely. "Look at me. We belong together. We're Cleo and Deuce, and nothing changes that." She stood on her tiptoes to kiss him on the cheek.

But Deuce wasn't so sure. It was one thing to be Cleo's boyfriend at Monster High and another altogether to go with her royal family on a fancy trip to Boo York. How would he manage? How would he cope with that beard? He'd have to think of something.

# CHAPTER 4

# All the Ghouls Are Going!

Across the room, Cleo and Deuce were putting down their lunch trays with Draculaura. Frankie hurried over to them. "Ooh! Hey, Cleo!" she called out. "Is it true? You're going to Boo York! I would give my right arm to go to Boo York!" With that, her right arm actually did fall off, and Frankie caught it before it hit the floor. She reattached it. "Oops!"

Cleo didn't even notice. She had just realized something. "Well," she said slowly. "You know, Frankie…my dad did say I could bring a friend… or two."

Draculaura gasped. "I'm a friend or two!"

"Oh, Cleo," sighed Clawdeen, sitting down at the table. "I *have* to go to Boo York. The fashion scene there is to die for."

Operetta, daughter of the Phantom of the Opera, popped up behind Cleo. "I hear that in Boo York they play music on every street corner." She smiled at her friend. "You know...just sayin.'"

"Boo York?" said Catty, sitting down with the ghouls. "Maybe that's where I'll find my music."

Cleo threw up her hands, her gold bangles jingling. "Okay, okay, I have decided."

All the ghouls froze in anticipation. Who would get to go? Who was Cleo going to pick? As Cleo looked from one ghoul to another, her heavily-lined eyes narrowed. "The ghoul going to Boo York," she announced at last, "is...ALL OF YOU!"

The Creepateria was filled with thrilled cheers and squeals of excitement.

"I have to pack!"

"What should I bring?"

"Boo York, here we come!"

Deuce scratched his head. "Are you sure about this?" he asked Cleo. "Your dad said only a friend or two."

"Hey, I can handle Daddy. Look at them!" replied Cleo breezily. "They love me! I'm Cleo de Nile, and I've got to give the people what they want."

Catty looked down at the scribbles for songs in the notebook in front of her. "They say that whatever you're looking for, you can find it in Boo York!"

All the ghouls sighed, picturing the skyscrapers and bright lights of the famous city. Clawdeen was imagining the fashion shows and the models and the runways she was going to see. Draculaura wanted to visit all the tourist sites—from the Monster of Liberty to Times Scare. Operetta could already hear the music from violinists on the subways to Bloodway stars belting out show tunes.

"You can find it all in Boo York," murmured Catty. "You can find what you are looking for." She thought of her wish on the comet. Was love waiting for her in

Boo York? Was her voice there to be found? Maybe, just maybe it was.

Cleo clapped her hands, reminding everyone who was making this trip possible. Not only would she bring her boyfriend but she'd bring her ghoulfriends too.

"You are all invited; come with me now. I'll take you to the greatest city unearthed!"

Everyone cheered. They were going to Boo York, together!

# CHAPTER 5

## On Bloodway

**T**he scareplane dipped through the clouds, and the ghouls looked out the windows to see Boo York beneath them at last. The city rose up closer and closer, and the plane touched down. A fleet of limos whisked the ghouls across the Spooklyn Bridge toward the heart of the city. Cars and taxis honked around them. The ghouls stared in amazement at the shopwindows and the crowded streets. "*Big city, bright lights. On our way to living the city life,*" sang the ghouls.

The limos pulled up in front of a fancy hotel, and gargoyles in bellhop caps zipped forward to unload a mountain of luggage.

Cleo held out her credit card to one of the bellboys. *"Oh yeah, I'm ready, gonna rock this place."*

Cleo took Deuce by the hand, and the ghouls followed them down the avenue to get an up-close look at everything. Banners stretched across the street announcing the arrival of the once-in-thirteen-hundred-years comet, and kids passed them wearing comet T-shirts and comet baseball hats. Everyone was gearing up for the big day.

Clawdeen wanted to check out the fashions at once. "Ghouls, we have to stop in that boo-tique!"

Without a moment's hesitation, they all rushed in. *"Me and my ghouls gonna run this town. We're gonna break the ground when we come around. Me and my ghouls gonna hit the scene. We're gonna make real life out of our dreams,"* sang the ghouls. They were trying on everything and giving one another a fashion show in the changing rooms. They snapped photos of each other to post online.

Arms linked and singing with happiness, the ghouls boarded the subway, heading to the Forty-Second Screech station. *"City streets never sleep. Let's hit the town every day of the week.*

*"Call out my name. I'll be center stage. We're on our way. C'mon, don't be late because this is the life. Sittin' pretty in the city. Yeah, this is the life."*

Their train groaned to a halt, and the ghouls and Deuce skipped out of the subway station into Times Scare. Huge screens flashed with advertisements for all the hit shows. *West Side Gory*! *Avenue Boo*! *Dreamghouls*! *Gory Poppins*! *Screamy Todd*! There was so much to see! There was so much to do! A street rapper was dazzling the crowds with his rapid-fire lyrics. His dark eyes glittered, and he grinned when he saw the ghouls. Draculaura snapped a photo of him and the rapper stopped, staring at Catty.

A Ghoulhound bus came to a stop by the curb. Out stepped a beautiful, earnest Jersey moth named Luna Mothews. She spun around in joy and tossed her hat into the air and caught it.

"Boo York City, here I am!" she announced in a lovely voice.

Draculaura stepped forward. "Hi, I'm Draculaura."

"Luna Mothews. Nice to meet you."

"And these are my ghoulfriends from Monster High," said Draculaura, introducing them.

Luna shook Draculaura's hand enthusiastically, and her suitcases fell to the ground. She giggled. "Nice to meet ya!"

"First time in Boo York?" Draculaura asked.

Luna gazed with wonder at the theater marquees. "Y'know I'll always be a Boo Jersey ghoul at heart, but I'm a moth and the bright lights of Bloodway are my flame! I've been working really hard, and one day you'll see me up onstage singing my heart out and my name will be up there on those signs!"

Luna fluttered into the air with excitement and bumped into a bored feline.

"Meow!" yowled the werecat.

Cleo whirled around. "Toralei!" she said with shock, recognizing their Monster High classmate. "What are you doing in Boo York City?"

"Whaaat?" asked Toralei. The stylish werecat

smiled smugly at Cleo. "Your sister, Nefera, invited me."

Nefera sidled up to Toralei, grinning. "Admit it, sister," she said to Cleo. "Having Toralei around always makes things more exciting."

Toralei purred. "I know I can make it here on Bloodway, and I can sing rings around you, little moth girl." She began yowling at the top of her lungs in the middle of Times Scare. Tires screeched. A car crashed.

Luna covered her ears. "Wow, huh, no. Not so much."

But Toralei didn't care. "See you in show business. 'Course you'll have to buy a ticket." She laughed.

Toralei stepped into a waiting limo.

Frankie handed Luna her luggage. "Good luck on Bloodway, Luna."

"Thanks," said Luna. "But in theater we say *break a leg*." A bright light caught Luna's attention and with a moth's perfect instincts, she flew toward it, mesmerized.

The ghouls linked arms and danced down the street together, taking in the energy and the dazzle of the city. Taxis honked, friends called out to one another, and music blasted from every street corner.

"There are so many talented performers everywhere!" gushed the ghouls.

A huge crowd was clustered around a robot DJ making electronic music right there on the sidewalk.

"Hey, look at that!" exclaimed Clawdeen.

In front of the robot was a holographic turntable, and she was spinning discs with wild abandon. The crowd cheered as one song ended with a flourish, and another song began. Lights pulsed and flashed around the DJ. Everyone started dancing. When she was done, the crowd cheered, and the robot DJ took a bow.

Frankie loved it. "That was amazing! Voltageously electric!" The bolts on her neck sparked.

The DJ's turntable vanished, and she bowed to the ghouls. "Thanks! You ghouls from out of town?"

"Monster High, actually," said Draculaura.

"Welcome to Boo York. My name's Elle Eedee." With a wave of her hand, she created a flourish of electronic notes.

Cleo stepped forward dramatically. "Well, I'm Cleo de Nile...of *the* De Niles."

"Ah!" said Elle, recognizing the name. "You must be here for that gala I'm gonna DJ tomorrow night. That comet must be super important. I heard the Ptolemys are hosting that gala."

Cleo gasped. In all the excitement, she had forgotten she was here with her family and not just her friends. She had obligations. She had important places to be. "Oh. My. Ra! I forgot. Nefera and I are supposed to be at Ptolemy Tower this afternoon for a meet and greet. We'll have to catch up with you ghouls later. C'mon, Deuce." She grabbed her boyfriend by the arm.

"You know," gulped Deuce. "I could just skip the…" But Cleo was already dragging him down the street.

A slug monster passed, pushing a huge cart of comet souvenirs down the street. It was overflowing with comet bobble heads, comet baseball hats, comet jewelry, comet T-shirts, and even stuffed comets.

"Getcha comet shirts here!" shouted the slug. "Show 'em you saw da comet by wearing a T-shirt." Boo Yorkers were crowding around the cart, handing him wads of cash.

"Whoa!" gushed Frankie. "Boo York is so exciting! There's so much to do and see!"

Catty's eyes were sparkling. "It's overwhelming. It's giving me ideas!"

"Ideas? Ideas for what?" asked Draculaura.

Catty blushed. Maybe it was time to confide in her friend. "I haven't been able to write new songs," she admitted. "I don't know what to write about. I just can't find my music."

A guitar-playing beast strolled past them, strumming and singing.

"If you can't find it in Boo York, it doesn't exist!" Frankie giggled.

Draculaura agreed. "Perhaps you can end your frighter's block. You'll find your music!"

Catty looked around her. It wasn't just music she needed. It was love. "A ghoul can dream," she whispered. "A ghoul can dream."

# CHAPTER 6

# The Mummy in the Golden Mask

Cleo held up her hand to hail a cab, but the yellow cars streamed past without stopping.

"Yo! Taxi," called out Deuce to no avail.

"Stop, please!" commanded Nefera, but none of them did. "What does it take to get a taxi in this town? Ugh! Don't they know who I am?"

A polished rat, chatting into her iCoffin, stepped in front of Cleo. "So I told the manager, 'Listen guy, I may be lactose intolerant, but I know cheesy when I smell it.'" She laughed as she raised her hand. A cab immediately screeched to a halt in front of her.

"How'd you do that?" asked Deuce, stepping forward.

The elegant rat waved her hat. "Go ahead. I'll get the next one."

"Thanks!" said Cleo, relieved.

Cleo, Nefera, and Deuce slid into the backseat.

"Do you know how to get to Ptolemy Tower?" asked Nefera. "We're in a hurry."

The cab driver, a grumpy werewolf, grumbled. "Sure. We'll take Howlston Street."

The rat, who had been watching, leaned in through the open window. "At this time of day? Are you crazy?" She slid into the backseat. "Scooch."

"You're gonna take Spectral Park West to Hexington Avenue," she ordered the cab driver.

Cleo was impressed. "You know a lot about Boo York."

"Upper Beast Side, born and raised," she said. "My family helped build this crazy maze of a city. The name's Mouscedes."

Nefera extended her hand across the squished backseat. "I'm Nefera."

"The name's Mouscedes. Mouscedes King."

Having a friend so familiar with the city could prove useful, thought Nefera.

With a jolt, the cabby peeled out into the street and wove in and out traffic until he pulled up in front of a magnificent golden tower. Cleo and Nefera raced toward the revolving doors of the building, and Deuce followed reluctantly.

Ramses was standing in the lobby, checking his watch. He was annoyed.

"Sorry we're late!"

"Hi, Daddy!"

Deuce bobbed his head. "Yo, Mr. D...."

Without a word, Ramses ushered them in to a waiting express elevator. As soon as the door was shut, Ramses exploded. "Late?! We have a meeting with the Ptolemys, the most powerful mummy family in all of Boo York, and you are *late*? If you weren't my daughters, I'd place a curse on you!"

The elevator doors opened to reveal a grand penthouse office that sat like a glass pyramid on top of the building. It was decorated in full Egyptian style. Ramses pulled himself together. Standing right in front of him was Amuncommon Ptolemy, the queen of Boo York and one of the most powerful mummies in the whole world. She was draped in gems and gold jewelry, and beside her was her son, Seth Ptolemy, wearing a golden mask that covered his entire face and made him look exactly like King Tut. It was all very fashionable.

With an elegant flourish of his robes, Ramses bent down on one knee and bowed his head. The ghouls barely recognized their furious father from a moment ago.

"Madame Ptolemy," said Ramses in his most ceremonial voice, "forgive me, please, my daughters are—"

"Late?" interrupted Madame Ptolemy. She clicked her tongue. "A pity you don't seem to have control over your children. My Seth would never be tardy for an appointment, would you, Seth?"

The gold-masked boy stepped forward. "No, Mother."

Deuce wondered how he could stand wearing that mask. That golden beard Cleo had put on him had been awful enough.

Cleo rolled her eyes. "Oh boy," she muttered.

Ramses was shaking Seth's hand vigorously. "A pleasure and an honor to meet you, Seth Ptolemy. They call you the prince of Boo York…" Ramses glared at his daughters. "Ahem," he coughed.

"Hello," said Nefera politely.

"Hey," said Cleo.

Madame Ptolemy, however, was staring at Deuce. "And you've brought a…friend?" she said, turning up her nose.

But Deuce wasn't exactly paying attention. He was wearing his earbuds and listening to rap music so loudly that it filtered into the penthouse. When he noticed everyone staring at him, he gave them the thumbs-up. But he could tell Ramses was furious. "Um…sup, Ms. P.…Ms. T.…um, Ms. Ptolemy." He stepped forward to give Madame Ptolemy a fist bump, and the queen glared at him.

Ramses's lip quivered with fury. A black cat sauntered out from behind a desk and hissed at Deuce. Deuce knew he was messing up, but he just didn't know how to make things better.

Madame Ptolemy shook her head. "Is that what the kids today are calling music, then? Dreadful. Am I right, Seth?" she asked, turning to her son.

"Terrorific noise, Mother," he said snobbishly.

Deuce coughed, aware he'd made a fool of himself.

Ramses sneered at him. "I'm sorry we are late, terribly…"

"No matter," said Madame Ptolemy. She waved her hand dismissively. "Unfortunately, I must make my next appointment, but I expect our families will become quite close at tomorrow night's gala." She eyed Nefera and raised an eyebrow quizzically. "Until tomorrow night, the night of the comet."

She took a final glance around the room and noticed Deuce kneeling next to a remarkably lifelike statue of a cat. Now where had that come from? She didn't remember it being in the room before.

Cleo, realizing what had happened, glared at Deuce.

Deuce adjusted his sunglasses. Being able to turn everything you looked at into stone could really be a problem sometimes. This was one of those times.

# CHAPTER 7

# Spectral Science

**H**igh above Monster High, the comet glowed and pulsed. Ghoulia was studying it from her iCoffin while she ate lunch in the Creepateria. Satellites were hovering around it. Suddenly, one of the satellites collided with the comet, and the bright orb spun and spiraled in a completely different direction.

Ghoulia groaned, putting down her drink. She picked up her laptop and raced out of the room. She dashed toward the elevator, pushed the button to head down to the catacombs, and quickly reapplied her lipstick.

The elevator door slid open to the laboratory. Ghoulia had an entire system of computers rigged up

at a worktable. She put her laptop down near them
and clicked on the power button. The large screen
on the computer glowed. The image of the comet
appeared.

Ghoulia gasped. It was just as bad as she thought.
It was headed right toward Earth!

Abbey Bominable, the confident yeti daughter
of the Abominable Snowman, peeked into the lab.
"Hello, Ghoulia. What is happening on computer?"

Ghoulia was typing furiously on her laptop. Abbey
studied the screen. The comet was zooming closer and
closer to Earth.

"Oh!" she exclaimed. "So comet knocked out of orbit is now heading toward Earth. Hmm, is that bad?"

Ghoulia nodded her head, trying to control her panic. She threw up her hands as if a giant bomb was exploding.

"Blow up the world?" Abbey's pale face was paler than ever. "But you can fix it, right?"

Ghoulia gulped and looked at the screen. That was the question. Could she stop the comet before it was too late?

# CHAPTER 8

## The Reluctant Mummy

**N**efera exited her hotel and got inside of a waiting limo. Sitting in the dark, waiting for her, was her father. One of his clawlike hands rested on a bejeweled cane.

"You wanted to see me?" Nefera asked.

Ramses cleared his throat. "Nefera, what do you know about the great comet that will pass over us tomorrow? Do you understand its importance to our Egyptian scaritage?"

Nefera glanced up through the skylight in the roof at the glowing orb poised over the Boo York skyline. It seemed to follow them as they drove. Nefera shrugged and reapplied her lipstick. "I understand it got me a free trip to Boo York."

Ramses shook his head. "Centuries ago, a small piece of that comet broke away and landed in the Sa-horror Desert. Our people found it. They found the comet crystal."

"Right," said Nefera impatiently. She knew this story already. "That rock thing we're gonna see tomorrow night at the gala."

"That rock thing," growled Ramses, "has a magic inside of it. Any promise made in the presence of the crystal when the comet is above becomes a real and unbreakable truth. Once made, it cannot be undone."

"So," said Nefera, barely interested, "no take-backsies."

She looked out the window at all the boo-tiques she wanted to visit. It was late at night, and the city was quiet and dark. The Ptolemy logo was everywhere, on buildings and billboards and advertisements of all kinds. A neon logo was reflected in a puddle and the limo drove through it, sending splashing water up over the curb.

Ramses continued speaking. "After the comet's power was discovered, it became customary for the most important royal betrothal ceremonies to be

performed under the light of that comet. Its power would make the couple's promise permanent."

Nefera was barely listening. She pulled out her compact to reapply her lip gloss. "This is all very interesting, Daddy," she yawned, "but what does any of it have to do with me?"

The limo slid into a parking place in front of the Ptolemy Tower. A black-suited, dog-headed Anubis guard rushed over to open the door. Ramses extended his hand to help Nefera out of the limo. He looked up at the tower, eyeing its gold magnificence.

"Do you see all of this? The money? The power?" he asked in a hushed voice so only Nefera could hear. "What if I told you that all this power could be ours? It's as simple as making a promise. The Ptolemys and the De Niles will be as one."

Ramses guided Nefera through the revolving

doors, and when the guards were distracted, he pulled out a tiny amulet that sent a magic spark into the control panel of the executive elevator. It almost seemed as though he and Nefera were doing something top secret and undercover.

Quietly, when the elevator doors slid open, Ramses led Nefera into the empty penthouse. The eyes of the cat statue followed them. It hissed at them through gritted teeth. In the center of the room was a glowing replica of the whole city of Boo York made out of magical sand. With his cane, Ramses traced the path the comet would follow over the city. "Tomorrow night under the light of the comet, you and Seth Ptolemy will make a promise to each other. A promise of betrothal. A promise to become the prince of Boo York's queen. A promise that will join our families together and create a dynasty!"

The more her dad spoke, the more horrified Nefera felt. As the eldest daughter, she was already destined to inherit the De Nile throne. Wasn't that enough? There was no way she could hide her disgust at marrying the gold-masked Seth Ptolemy.

"A dynasty!" continued Ramses, moving his hands over the glowing city. "Just think what we have to gain. Oceans of money, monuments, buildings, the De Nile cartouche inscribed everywhere just like the Ptolemy logo. Just promise to be with Seth, and all of your dreams will come true."

It's true that money and power were tempting to Nefera. She was a De Nile after all.

Ramses could tell that his daughter was considering it. "It's that simple," he said softly. "You and Seth promise to be with each other for all time, and the De Nile family will achieve true power."

At the mention of Seth's name, Nefera shook her head. "But…I don't want to be with that Seth kid. He's weird."

"All right," agreed Ramses. "He is a little weird. But you are a De Nile. You will obey; you have no choice." He leaned in close. "And think about all the power you will have if you just go through with the ceremony."

Nefera was torn. It was hard to give up a dynasty, but it was even harder to think about marrying Seth. But then it hit her. "What if there was another way?"

"I'm listening," said Ramses.

Light from the surrounding skyscrapers cast an enormous shadow of Nefera across the floor of the penthouse. "I want the wealth and power," she told her father. "The De Niles and the Ptolemys should join together and form a dynasty. But why should I have to do all the betrothal and promising?" She smiled sweetly at her father. "Isn't that what younger sisters are for?"

Ramses stroked his chin, intrigued.

Nefera continued. "Make Cleo promise to be with Seth Ptolemy. She'd be a real ghoul of the people. She could be a great ruler...with our guidance."

Nefera began crooning a sultry song describing the power she and her father could wield over Cleo. They would sit on thrones; they would reign over a great empire. "*We'll take over the world, you and I together. Nobody can stop us!*"

Ramses's eyes glittered. "*Empire, empire,*" he sang along. "*Building us an empire!*"

"*All I want is everything,*" trilled Nefera, "*'cause we're kings and queens, why pretend to be anything less. I'm a goddess.*"

"*Don't be modest,*" Ramses joined in. "*When we run this kingdom, it's gonna be monstrous.*"

They were going to reign over everything! They were going to take over everything! No one could stop them from building a mighty empire.

Except for Cleo.

"What if Cleo doesn't cooperate?" asked Ramses.

Nefera smirked. "Oh, you're right. I've just got to get Deuce out of the picture first."

Ramses clapped his hands. Not only would he rule the world through his daughter—but he'd get Deuce out of their lives too. What could be better?

Nefera pulled out her iCoffin and called up Mouscedes.

Mouscedes was looking in a window at a glittering comet-inspired gown when she answered her phone. "Nefera?"

Nefera and her father slipped back onto the elevator while she explained her plan to Mouscedes. "Listen, I need someone with your class to help me set up a brunch tomorrow morning. It has to be very fancy. A really elegant, high-brow affair."

She winked at her father. She had this. She knew exactly what to do. Cleo wasn't going to break up with Deuce just because her father told her to. No. Instead, Nefera was going to show her sister how a royal De Nile should never, ever date a gorgon.

# CHAPTER 9

## A Monstrous Mess

Nefera and Mouscedes looked around the dining room. A banquet table shaped like an all-seeing eye was covered in delicacies. Gargoyle waiters in white suit jackets hurried past, getting everything ready for the brunch.

When the ghouls arrived, all dressed up in their favorite fashions, they were amazed.

"Oh my ghoul!" gushed Clawdeen. "Look at this view! I think I can see Boo Jersey from here." As she took a seat at a table, a gargoyle held out her chair for her.

"Nefera, this is too much," Frankie said. "Thank you for putting this brunch together."

Cleo's eyes narrowed. Something was wrong here, but she couldn't figure out what it was. "Yes," she said suspiciously, "why *did* you put this brunch together?"

Nefera smiled innocently. "What? I can't throw together a little pre-gala breakfast soiree for my sister and her friends? Besides, Mouscedes did most of the planning. That ghoul's got connections."

Mouscedes brushed it off with a giggle and a squeak.

"Ah!" announced Nefera. "Here comes our guest of honor!"

Seth Ptolemy appeared at the entrance to the dining room. He was wearing a little cape and his gold mask gleamed.

Nefera led him to a chair next to Cleo. "Ghouls, meet Seth Ptolemy. But then I don't have to tell you who the prince of Boo York is." She smiled. "Seth, you'll be sitting here next to Cleo."

Seth flipped his cape as he sat down, and Cleo rolled her eyes.

"Wait a minute," said Cleo, looking around the room. "Where's Deuce? You invited him too, right?"

"Oh, he'll be here," said Nefera brightly. "I'm counting on it."

Seth turned to Cleo and spoke in a stiff, formal

voice. "Do you like Spookfear's sonnets?" he asked.

Cleo shrugged. "Is that some kind of Boo York band or something?"

"Oh my no!" gasped Seth. "We Ptolemys don't care for wild modern music. I am talking about poetry." He pulled out a notebook. "I write poetry," he explained.

Cleo could not hide her boredom. "Wonderful," she said without looking at him.

This was enough encouragement, and Seth began reciting poetry to Cleo. "If music be the food of love, play on. Play on. And again."

Cleo felt like she had been listening to him drone on for a thousand years when Deuce finally arrived.

For some strange reason, Deuce was dressed for the pool. He was wearing a bathing suit, a snorkel, a mask, and fins. He was carrying an inflatable raft.

"You're late!" hissed Cleo. Deuce looked completely confused.

Cleo raised an arched eyebrow. "And what are you wearing? The invitation said formal attire."

"I thought it was a pool party," explained Deuce.

Cleo was irritated. "Oh, Deuce, are you doing this on purpose?" She sighed. "Never mind, just come sit down." She pulled the fake beard out of her purse and stuck it on his chin. Deuce's snakes hissed at it.

The ancient waiter approached them. "I'm sorry, sir, but a suit jacket is required for all gentlemen to enter."

"He doesn't have one," Cleo said, knowing there was no way Deuce had brought a suit jacket to a pool party.

The waiter snapped his fingers. A host of dog-headed Anubis waiters rushed over and removed Deuce's swimming gear. One of them held up a jacket. It was enormous, and it was plaid. "This is the only loaner jacket we have," said the waiter.

When Deuce put it on, the sleeves hung down to his knees.

Meanwhile, Nefera sauntered by and slipped a wad of bills into the waiter's jacket pocket.

In his oversize plaid jacket and swimming trunks, Deuce looked ridiculous. The ghouls tried not to laugh as they finished their meals.

"Hey, everyone," said Deuce, sitting down. "Don't we look nice this morning?" He reached for his water glass but knocked it over because his hand was lost in his sleeve.

"Oh no, my poetry!" Seth grabbed his notebook and dried it off.

"Sorry. Major brunch foul," Deuce apologized.

Nefera smirked.

"This is amazing," Toralei grinned.

A slew of waiters marched into the dining room and placed domed trays in front of each diner.

Mouscedes clapped her hands. "And now for a Boo York specialty—scary cherries flambé!"

The waiters lifted the covers of the plates, revealing the flaming desserts. Nefera leaned close to Deuce and whispered, "Oh no! The food! It's on fire! Do something!"

Deuce threw up his hands and tipped the dish in front of him over to extinguish the flames—but the entire tablecloth caught on fire. Deuce leaped up and grabbed a fire extinguisher and blasted the table. Foam was covering the food, the waiters, and the ghouls in their best dresses. As Deuce tried to put the fire out, Nefera stuck out a foot and tripped him, sending him sprawling across the room.

Deuce's special gorgon sunglasses fell off and beams from his eyes flew right at the head waiter, turning him to stone. The snakes on his head hissed and shook off the foam from the fire extinguisher.

Everyone was screaming as the fire alarm rang loudly and a crew of monster firemen burst into the room carrying hoses. Deuce quickly put his sunglasses back on and looked around the room. He was embarrassed when he realized what a catastrophe he'd created. Nefera looked on smugly as Cleo, who appeared to be totally cool and composed, sat down beside him.

"Deuce," she said icily, "the scary cherries are supposed to be on fire." Without another word, she stormed out of the dining room, leaving a trail of foam behind her.

Deuce put his head in his hands. Even his snakes were embarrassed. A waiter handed him his snorkel and fins.

Nefera brought him over a bowl of cherries. "Here," she said sweetly, "I scraped out a little spot that wasn't covered in toxic safety foam."

Deuce didn't look up. "I don't know why I keep doing that."

"Going all crazy with a fire extinguisher? This is a regular thing for you?" Nefera asked.

"No, I mean, I don't know why I keep embarrassing Cleo."

Nefera nodded her head. "Oh well, let's face it. Cleo is an Egyptian princess. And you are, well, Deuce. You come from two very different worlds."

Deuce knew she was right. "She deserves better," he said sadly.

Nefera tried not to grin. She placed a comforting hand on Deuce's shoulder. "The way I see it, you could stay with Cleo for a little while longer, pretending to be good enough for her, or you could set her free so she can move on with her life. And find someone truly worthy of Egyptian royalty." Nefera stood up. "I'm sure you'll make the right decision. If you love her, you'll leave her."

Confident in the success of her plan, Nefera left Deuce alone with his humiliation. He poked at the cherries with a spoon. Nefera was right. He was out of place. He knew it. Cleo knew it. Her father knew it. Everyone knew it now. It was time for him to make a change. If only he didn't like Cleo so much…

# CHAPTER 10

# Music from the Stars

Deep in the catacombs of Monster High, Ghoulia was using all her smarts to try to save the world. She pulled up screens of numbers, studied maps, and clicked through equation after equation, trying to find a solution.

Abbey shook her head. "Comet path is unstable?"

Ghoulia zoomed in on the comet. She typed in a series of numbers and a line stretched from the comet—right to Boo York.

"The comet will crash into Boo York City at midnight?" Abbey's eyes widened.

Ghoulia groaned.

*But that's where our friends are*! Ghoulia realized.

Both ghouls looked at the screen. There had to be a way to stop the comet—but could they do it before midnight? Ghoulia's hands flew across the keyboard.

Abbey watched, impressed. "What is that you are doing? You're hacking into satellite system to investigate? Very clever!"

The screen began beeping as a satellite slowly deviated from its orbit—and headed toward the comet. Its signal beam was flashing.

In Boo York, the ghouls had no idea what danger they were in. They were happy to be tourists. Draculaura was checking off the sites they'd visited in her guidebook. "Okay, so far we've seen Ptolemy Tower, Times Scare, and the Vampire State Building. I say next we hit the Monster of Liberty before the gala tonight."

They were standing on a crowded street near a pizza shop. A small werewolf boy dropped a quarter into a mechanical comet and hopped on to ride it back and forth like a horse. An actor dressed up like a gigantic pizza was handing out flyers. "Get your creeparoni pizza here!"

At the sound of the actor's voice, the ghouls recognized who was inside the pizza costume. It was Luna.

"Hey ghouls!" she exclaimed, recognizing them at the same time.

"Luna?" Frankie asked.

"Something about you looks different," noted Clawdeen. "Don't tell me. Haircut?"

"Ha, very funny." Luna laughed. "Yeah, I know I look silly, but, hey, technically I'm now a working actor in Boo York City."

The ghouls were just about to tell her about the brunch fiasco when they were distracted by a pulsing buzz. Elle Eedee, the robot DJ, was spinning down the street in a kind of trance, emitting all kinds of electronic sounds and static.

"Losing signal…searching again…changing frequency," muttered Elle, oblivious to the world around her. She pulsed and buzzed and whirred in a daze.

What no one on Earth knew was that deep inside
the comet an alarm had gone off. A signal from the
satellite had activated something…or someone. A
sleeping figure in what looked like the cockpit of a
spaceship began to emit ethereal musical notes.

All Ghoulia and Abbey could hear was static and
buzzing. Ghoulia pressed a button on her computer
screen, and the feedback stopped.

Frankie took Elle by the shoulders and shook her. "Are
you okay? What's happening?"

Elle blinked her eyes, confused. "I don't know. It
was like…a song in my head. It was faint and unclear,
like a bad transmission from somewhere." She blinked
again. "Is that ghoul dressed like a pizza?"

"Is that really important?" asked Luna.

Elle paced back and forth, upset by the weird
buzzing feeling in her head. "I've got to figure out

what it means. The sound is still inside of me." She waved her hands to make her holographic turntables appear and tried to re-create the pulsing, whirring sound, but she couldn't.

Back at Monster High, Ghoulia wasn't having any luck, either. The comet wasn't slowing down! It was still headed right for Boo York. It would still strike at midnight. What else could she do? There had to be something. There just had to be.

# CHAPTER 11

## Heartbreak Horror

Cleo was picking out a ball gown for the gala in her suite at the hotel. The plush room was littered with dresses. They were draped over the sphinx-shaped couch and scattered all over the floor. An Anubis guard was bringing in another rack for her to sample. But Cleo couldn't find just the right gown. She was so absorbed in her fashion emergency that she barely looked up when the guard let Deuce into the room.

"Oh good, you're here," she said distractedly. She held up two gowns. "Which do you like better? Burnt-at-the-stake sienna or haunted-forest green?"

Deuce looked down at his feet, stone-faced and

heartbroken. "They're both nice, I guess."

Cleo sighed. "That's not very helpful. What are you wearing tonight to the gala?"

Deuce took a deep breath. "I'm not going to the gala."

Cleo assumed he was joking. "Kinda hard for you to be my date if you're not at the gala…" But then she saw Deuce's face. Her eyes widened in alarm. "Deuce is this about what happened at brunch?"

"It's not about brunch. It's about everything." It all came rushing out of him. "Cleo, look at us. This was never going to last. We're just too different."

The gowns fell from Cleo's hands. She felt like the wind had been knocked out of her. "What are you saying?"

"You're Egyptian royalty, and I love you too much to hold you back."

Shocked, Cleo sat down on the edge of the couch. "I can't believe what I'm hearing."

But Deuce was on a roll now. "I can see the way people look at us when we walk down the street together. What's a ghoul like her doing with a fool like him? You're elegant. I'm grungy. You're sophisticated. I'm a brute. I'm releasing you to go on with your life."

"Stop this!" Cleo ordered. "I won't let you."

"There's nothing you can say to change my mind. Look deep down, and you'll realize you've known it all along too. That's right—we're wrong together."

Deuce turned on his heel to leave, but Cleo was up and standing in front of the door. "I've heard enough. We are not breaking up. We are the power couple of Monster High. I don't care what anyone says—and neither should you." Cleo spoke from her heart and had never looked more regal.

Deuce realized that Cleo wasn't going to give in, and he knew he had to do something drastic to show her just how serious he was. In one swift movement, he snatched off the golden beard Cleo kept making him wear and threw it across the room. "You see this? This isn't me."

The beard flew into the fireplace with a clang and began to melt. Cleo shrieked, in a complete state of shock.

"I am not part of this world," continued Deuce. "I never will be."

Cleo dropped to her knees and started to cry. She loved Deuce, and she could not believe he was being so cruel.

Deuce felt terrible, but he steeled himself—he had to do this. "I've said all I have to say. Don't make me say it again. We're not Cleo and Deuce anymore." He stormed out of the room, and Cleo threw herself onto the floor, sobbing.

Out in the hallway, Deuce stopped, listening to her cries. Now that she couldn't see him, his face softened and tears welled up in his eyes. He was doing this for Cleo. *Because* he loved her. Someday she'd understand. As he pushed the button to go down in the elevator, Nefera stepped out of the shadows.

"Aww," she said sympathetically. "Don't cry, Deucy. You did what you had to do." She ushered him on to the elevator and as soon as the doors were shut, she clapped her hands and cackled. "And now I'm going to make my sister agree to perform the Promise Ceremony tonight. Ooooh! This is fun!"

Back in the suite, Cleo was sitting in front of her vanity. She was devastated. Nefera began brushing her hair, comforting her.

Tears were still rolling down Cleo's cheeks. "He just stormed out of the room. I don't understand it. It's like it came out of nowhere."

"Oh, Cleo!" sighed Nefera. "This didn't come out of nowhere. I feel like this is partly my fault."

Cleo swiveled around to look at her sister.

"I should have made you understand what your family and friends have known all along," Nefera continued. "You and Deuce were never meant to be. We all saw the hieroglyphics on the wall. You deserve to be with someone...powerful. Someone who can give you everything you deserve."

Cleo just sniffled—she didn't want anyone but Deuce. Nefera smiled at her sweetly, stroking her hair. "You deserve to be with someone like Seth Ptolemy."

Cleo's face dropped. "But I don't understand his poetry. He's just not right for me. No offense, Nefera, but I don't see that happening."

Nefera shrugged. "You didn't see Deuce breaking

up with you, either…" Her voice trailed off. She tried another tack. "Cleo, sooner or later you are going to realize this is a good thing. Without Deuce holding you back, there's no telling what kind of greatness you might find."

She shot Cleo a knowing grin before leaving Cleo to think about what she'd said.

Cleo sat for a long time by herself at the vanity. She looked at the melted gold beard in the fireplace, and she looked out the window where the all-seeing logo of the Ptolemy eye was blinking on and off on a neon sign.

# CHAPTER 12

## Catty Lands on Her Feet

The ghouls stepped out of the subway, and Draculaura consulted her travel guide. "According to this," she told the others, "the scary ferry to the Monster of Liberty should be just a little bit farther once we switch subway trains and. . ."

She stopped talking because she realized no one else was listening to her. The ghouls were mesmerized by a handsome rapper entertaining a crowd of commuters with his miraculous rhymes. It was the same boy they had seen the day before—Pharaoh.

Ghouls were squealing and screaming, "Pharaoh! Pharaoh!"

"*You are now rocking with the very best rapper from*

*around the way I wanna say HELLO."* He grinned. *"Hello!"*

Pharaoh grabbed knitting needles from an old lady and began drumming on garbage can lids and getting the crowd to help him make the music he needed. He was a whirling, dancing phenomenon.

*"Everybody calls me by my old name. Ugh. So lame. You can just call me Pharaoh."*

As he swung around, his eyes landed on Catty, and she smiled. He cocked an eyebrow. Suddenly, a smile of recognition lit up his face.

"I saw him earlier," said Catty, riveted by his performance.

"He's really good," Operetta replied.

Pharaoh's rhymes were exploding. They were propulsive, irresistible, and amazing. He was so talented. He didn't seem to need to take a breath. The crowd was cheering. A ghoul fainted. And the whole time Pharaoh never took his eyes off Catty.

Pharaoh held out his hand to her. *"All of you should stand up and dance, no sitting. Straight up out the tomb, big dreams on my mind, gotta find my way in this Boo York way of life,"* he rapped.

Catty opened her mouth and out came the purest

of notes and the sweetest of songs. "*It's the place we all wanna go. Be the star of the show. When you're out in Boo York, Boo York,*" she sang, "*a ghoul can find what she's looking for!*"

He rapped, she sang, and their performance was electric.

But Pharaoh and Catty didn't even know they were performing. It was as if the crowd and the city had disappeared and the two of them were the only monsters in the whole world. His deep rich voice harmonized perfectly with her lyrical vocals.

The crowd was snapping pictures and videos.

"It's Catty Noir!"

"It is!"

"Catty, Catty, over here! We love you!"

Still singing to each other, Catty and Pharaoh climbed the steps out of the subway station together. They never took their eyes off of each other. It was a dazzling duet. The crowd followed them, shouting encouragement.

"Okay, everyone, let's try to stay nice and orderly," Draculaura urged just as she was almost trampled— luckily she escaped by turning into a bat.

Out in an alley, Catty and Pharaoh were hiding

behind newspapers as the crowd raced past. When at last they were alone, Pharaoh leaned over and introduced himself. "Hey," he said sweetly, "I'm Pharaoh." As if Catty didn't already know!

Catty smiled. "Hi! I'm Catty Noir!"

"I know." Pharaoh laughed. "We sounded pretty good together."

A scream startled them. Another fan had noticed them, even behind their newspapers! Catty and Pharaoh dropped their newspapers and ran for it, the crowd in hot pursuit. Pharaoh grabbed Catty's arm and pulled her into a hidden alley.

"*Come with me*," he sang to her, reaching for her hand. Pharaoh pulled Catty away from the crowd and together they ran down the alley, laughing and singing. "This way! Let me show you MY town."

They slipped down another alley as the crowd roared past without seeing them. Pharaoh led Catty up a fire escape, and they watched their fans disappear down the street.

Catty watched, confused, as Pharaoh began climbing the fire escape. "Wait, we're going up?"

Pharaoh grinned. They were! Up and up, he took Catty to the top of the city. The wind whooshed through their hair. They jumped from one rooftop to another. Pharaoh slid down the railing of a giant advertisement and landed on another building.

"You are crazy!" Catty laughed.

"What's crazy," said Pharaoh, "is a famous pop star trying to walk down the street without getting recognized. C'mon. You can get anywhere you want in the city up here."

Catty took a deep breath, grabbed hold of the railing, and shut her eyes. Pharaoh caught her in his arms.

"Come on, we have a whole city to explore!" invited Pharaoh.

Catty had never been happier. "Well, then we better get started!"

"Hey, wait up!" Pharaoh dashed across a catwalk, and Catty sent a quick text to her friends so they wouldn't worry—and then she hurried after Pharaoh. Wherever he was going, she was going!

Down on the street, Frankie read Catty's text to the other ghouls. "She says she'll meet up with us at the comet gala tonight."

"Speaking of which," said Operetta, "we should probably head back and start getting ready."

Draculaura was disappointed. "But what about the Hauntson River Bridge?"

Clawdeen shook her head. "Sorry, Draculaura, there's just too much to see and do here. We can always come back for another visit."

"That's right," said Frankie. "It's not like Boo York is going anywhere."

Overhead, the comet pulsed and brightened.

# CHAPTER 13

## Satellite Games

At Monster High, Abbey was panicking and pointing at the computer screen. Ghoulia was typing as fast as she could, trying to control the satellites and divert the comet. Heath Burns and Manny Taur, two classmates of the ghouls, were passing by the laboratory and saw what was happening. Immediately they thought they knew what was going on. The ghouls were playing some cool new video game!

"Yes," Abbey directed Ghoulia. "Move satellites closer to investigate comet."

"Cool game!" Heath and Manny exclaimed together, peering at the screen.

"No!" shouted Abbey.

But Heath didn't listen. He grabbed Ghoulia's laptop and began pounding the keyboard. "Quit hoggin', Ghoulia. My turn!"

"I got next!" Manny announced.

Heath was pressing all kinds of command buttons. "Okay, so what do you do? Crash into the comet? Cool!"

Out in the darkness of space, the satellites veered and shifted. They were all headed right toward the comet!

Beep! Beep! Beep! The control panel, deep in the heart of the comet, was sensing danger. But the pilot or the passenger was fast asleep. Still, an automatic button sent a beam of pure music blasting toward the satellites, which flew off in different directions.

Abbey and Ghoulia watched in horror. But they didn't dare tell Manny and Heath what was really going on. They didn't want to alarm them.

"Holy smokes!" shouted Heath, excited. He pressed another command and sent a satellite back in the direction of the comet. He was going to destroy it and win.

Ghoulia pulled Abbey aside, whispering to her.

"Comets have defense systems?" Ghoulia had

explained to her that something very strange was going on.

Maybe the comet wasn't a comet at all. Maybe it was a. . .

"Spaceship!" exclaimed Abbey.

But what did that mean? Was it still going to crash into Boo York and destroy it? And what if the satellites destroyed the spaceship? What if someone was on board?

One of the satellites rotated. The comet blasted toward Earth.

Ghoulia grabbed the keyboard back. She had to figure out what to do!

"So spaceship means somebody inside, right?" realized Abbey.

Ghoulia acknowledged her with a groan.

Mr. Rotter poked his head into the laboratory. He couldn't believe what he was seeing! "Video games! On school grounds!"

Manny and Heath exchanged a worried glance. Were they in trouble again?

But Mr. Rotter was about to surprise them. "I love video games," he exclaimed. He high-fived Manny and sat down at the large computer monitor.

"Yeah!" said Manny. Maybe Mr. Rotter was cooler than he seemed.

Ghoulia barely noticed her teacher sitting down. She was focused on trying to find out more about the pilot of the comet. How could she do that?

Abbey was thinking out loud. "Maybe space pilot in deep frozen sleep. No big deal. In old country, we do this all the time."

As if on cue, Ghoulia's laptop screen showed a thermal scan of the comet. Deep in its heart was a figure, hunched over and fast asleep.

"So we wake pilot, we save world?" asked Abbey. "But how we do that?"

That was the question, but Ghoulia didn't know the answer...yet.

Deep inside the comet, the pilot stretched and yawned.

# CHAPTER 14

## Fright Night

**D**euce slouched as he walked down the street. He was so depressed he didn't even notice all the televisions in an electronic store he passed, each one showing a vampire dressed up in a giant, foam comet costume.

"Hey, Boo Yorker!" shouted the vampire retailer on the screens. "Have you got comet fever? I know I do! Crazy Deady here with a deal so good it only comes around once every thirteen hundred years." He laughed maniacally.

High above the street, Catty and Pharaoh were talking about music. They loved all of the same artists—Mummyford and Sons, Scaryanna Groan-day, Casta and the Spells.

Pharaoh gazed at Catty with wonder. "I can't remember the last time I got to spend any time with a real music lover like you."

"Your friends don't like music?" Catty asked.

"No. And my family can't stand it. They only like the oldies. Like from when Tut was young. They think my rapping is a waste of time."

Catty shook her head. "That's terrible."

"Hey," said Pharaoh, an idea coming to him. "If you like music, I've got a place you are really going to love."

An hour later, Pharaoh led Catty up a staircase, through a green hatch, and onto a green-hued balcony way above the city. The wind blew through Catty's pink-hued hair.

"Oh my ghoul!" she gushed as she took in the amazing view. "Where are we?"

Pharaoh held his finger to his lips. "Close your eyes and listen."

Catty listened, but she didn't know what she was supposed to hear. "All I hear is city noise."

"Ah," grinned Pharaoh, "but you're not really listening." He closed his eyes and began to bop to a hidden beat.

Catty shut her eyes, trying to feel it too. From far below in the city, she heard a train go by. She heard children, laughing and playing on a playground. She heard cars honking. She heard the bounce of a basketball. The city had its own rhythm. The city had its own beat. The city had its own song. "I hear music!" exclaimed Catty. She opened her eyes. "I've found my music!"

The lights of the city blinked softly, the strains of music floated upward. Catty and Pharaoh were falling in love, and they both knew it. Pharaoh felt like he could be himself with Catty. Catty felt a fluttering of excitement deep in her heart that she had never felt before. Catty began singing in tune with the music below, and Pharaoh joined her, rapping, sweetly professing his love. Their voices rose to the stars. There they were, singing their duet, nestled in the very crown of the Monster of Liberty.

Back in the hotel, the strains of orchestral music wafted through the open window of the ghouls' room. They were zipping up their dresses and curling their hair. They were putting on lipstick and spritzing perfume. Frankie carefully drew a line of blue shadow on her eyelid, just like an Egyptian. Clawdeen added another hot roller to her voluptuous mane. Operetta helped Draculaura with her lip gloss because Draculaura, being a vampire, couldn't see herself in the mirror. All dressed up at last, the ghouls spun and twirled in their ball gowns like they were on the runway.

Across town in a small, spare apartment, Luna was also getting dressed. Her wings fluttered with excitement. Mouscedes was picking out shoes at her elegant home on the Upper Beast Side. Elle was putting some last touches to her makeup and buffing her steel robot cheeks until they shone. Everyone was gearing up for the big night, the gala, the night of the comet. Boo York hadn't seen a night like this in 1,300 years!

The ghouls finished getting ready long before the limos were set to pick them up. They were just so excited.

Clawdeen checked her watch. "We still have like half an hour before we have to head down."

"So what do we do now?" Frankie wondered.

"More gala gown strutting?" Operetta suggested, and all the ghouls thought that was a perfect idea.

Alone in her suite, Cleo was not ready to go, however. Her ball gown hung in the corner. Tears stained her cheeks.

Nefera marched into her room, alarmed. "Cleo! What are you doing? Why aren't you dressed for the gala?"

"I'm too upset about Deuce," Cleo explained between sobs. "Who cares about galas? I'm not going."

Nefera wrung her hands. "You have to," she ordered. "You have to be there to promise…"

Cleo stared at her sister, waiting for her to finish, but Nefera realized her mistake and stopped speaking. She snapped her fingers, and a guard brought over a tray of makeup. Nefera began lining Cleo's eyes. "You have to go because you promised you would. Everybody's expecting you to be there. Your family. Your ghoulfriends. All the important Egyptians." She sat down beside her sister and wrapped an arm around her. "This is a very special night for us, Cleo. The night of the comet. You don't want to let everybody down—do you?"

Cleo stood up and walked over to the window. She sighed. "I'm Cleo de Nile, and I've got to give the people what they want." Listlessly, she began putting on her ball gown.

Just visible through the skyscrapers was the glowing green crown of the Monster of Liberty, where a new couple, falling deeply in love, was discovering their music together.

# CHAPTER 15

## Love Spells

The light of the comet bathed the city in a shimmering glow. Still up in the Monster of Liberty, Catty was scribbling song lyrics on a scrap of paper. Her heart was overflowing, and she had to express herself. The words were easy, the rhymes were easy, and the writing was effortless.

Pharaoh peeked over her shoulder playfully. "What are you writing? A song?"

"I don't know," admitted Catty. "It's just pouring out of me. Thoughts, feelings. I'm trying to get it all down."

Pharaoh noticed that she was almost out of paper

and tore off a scrap of one of his mummy bandages. "Here, you can write on this."

Catty smiled at him. "I haven't felt this inspired to write in a long time." She blushed. "So, where did you learn to rap like that?"

"I don't know how to tell you this, but…I'm a mummy!" Pharaoh laughed, holding up his arm so one of the bandages hung down. He wrapped it back around his wrist. "After a few tries, you start to get the hang of it."

"Hilarious," smiled Catty.

"Seriously, though," said Pharaoh, "I've always been able to do it. I think about how I feel, and it just comes out of me. Kinda like you and your writing just now."

Catty gazed adoringly at Pharaoh. "You are very good."

"I'm glad you got to hear it," beamed Pharaoh. "Because after tonight, I won't be rapping anymore."

Catty couldn't believe her ears. She was shocked. "What are you talking about? You can't quit!"

"Why not? You quit."

"Th-that's different," Catty stammered. "I stopped singing because I wasn't being true to myself. Because they were asking me to sing songs written by somebody else. But you, you sing from your heart. You've *found* your voice. Why would you give that up?"

Pharaoh took a deep breath as if there was so much he wanted to say but couldn't. "It's complicated."

"They offered me fame and money. They wanted to make me a pop queen of the world, and I gave it all up to try and find what you have." Catty looked up at the sky, and she noticed that the comet was closer than ever. She blinked, remembering that she had a gala to go to. She stood up hastily. "I have to get ready for the big comet gala at the museum."

"Did you say gala?" asked Pharaoh, his eyes darting back and forth.

"Yeah," answered Catty. "Why?"

Pharaoh shrugged. "No reason."

Catty went to climb back down the stairs. She turned back to Pharaoh before she left. "Think about what I said. I hope I get to see you again." She disappeared, leaving Pharaoh alone under the stars.

The hint of a smile turned up the corners of Pharaoh's mouth. He looked up at the comet. "Hmm," he murmured. "Maybe it is time to be true to myself."

# CHAPTER 16

## Freaky Feedback

Limousines were pulling up in front of the Museum of Unnatural History. Cameras were flashing. Well-dressed dignitaries in their best bandages and gowns were walking up the red carpet that led into the main hall. A huge banner with the comet on it was strung from pillar to pillar. The crowd outside the museum was all dressed up in comet gear and carrying comet signs.

Inside, Elle Eedee was working her turntable, playing a classy mix of ancient Egyptian music. The ghouls in their ball gowns strode in time to the beat, past the crowds, and into the gala.

"Totes fierce!" Clawdeen whispered to Frankie.

"Can you believe this?" said Draculaura to Catty.

"A fright to remember!" sighed Operetta.

Just after the ghouls arrived, a fanfare announced the guests of honor—Madame Ptolemy and her son, Seth. Seth tripped on the carpet coming in, and his mother shook her head. She nodded at Elle as she passed. "Very good. That's the kind of music we want to hear this evening. None of that other stuff. Isn't that right, Seth?"

"Yes, Mother," agreed Seth.

Elle plastered a smile on her face, trying to be polite.

The De Niles arrived, waving their hands at the crowd. Cleo held her head high even though her heart was breaking. Ramses and Nefera were just behind her, whispering.

"I presume there will be a Promise Ceremony later tonight with the Ptolemy boy?" asked Ramses.

"Of course, Father," smiled Nefera, reassuringly. "I've got Cleo exactly where I want her..."

Inside the rotunda, silk banners advertised the night of the comet. Well-dressed guests mingled beside exhibits about ancient Egypt. Spotlights picked out celebrities, and waiters passed by carrying trays of drinks. Up on the balcony was a small stage with a microphone. For a moment, the whole museum was plunged into total darkness and then across the domed ceiling flashed a spectacular light show. It was like being in a planetarium or even out in space.

Madame Ptolemy took the stage. "Hurtling through space, brimming with magical energy, the great comet only graces us with its mystical presence once every thirteen hundred years. And tonight, it visits us once more."

The ceiling projection showed the comet burning brightly above the pyramids. A line of mummies in profile began walking across the sky. In the middle of them was an otherworldly being, a kind of star child.

"Our ancestors believed the great comet was a gift from the others above," explained Madame Ptolemy. The star child shone alone on the ceiling. "A mysterious race of beings that live beyond the stars. Why did they send the comet? Is it a message? A peace offering? A warning? We don't know. But we do know that any promise made under the magic light of the comet cannot be broken."

The image of the star child dissolved and was replaced by a pair of mummies holding hands. A stream of light shone down on them from above.

Triumphantly, Madame Ptolemy continued, "And so we created the Promise Ceremony, where our children would commit to be together, forever joining their families to create powerful dynasties. Whatever is spoken in the presence of the comet will be for *all* time. And when the ceremony is complete, the comet leaves. But we have something to remind us that she'll be back again someday."

The light show revealed the comet in space and a small piece of it breaking off and plummeting to the earth. It crashed into the sands of ancient Egypt. Behind Madame Ptolemy, a black obelisk began to rise. Embedded in its pinnacle was the crystal itself. It

Cleo, Nefera, and Deuce show up to meet the Ptolemy family... just a little bit late!

"Big city, bright lights. On our way to living the city life," sing Cleo and the ghouls as they walk down the streets of Bloodway.

Madame Ptolemy and her son, Seth

Deuce tells Cleo he loves her too much to hold her back. Is Monster High's top couple really over?

"Sooner or later, you will realize this is a good thing," Nefera tells Cleo.

Nefera fumes after Seth reveals he is in love with Catty Noir!

Luna Mothews is destined to become the next big star on Bloodway!

Thanks to Astranova, the comet helps everyone find just what they're looking for in Boo York!

"Monster High is real!" Astranova tells her hexcited friends back at Ever After High, Apple White and Raven Queen.

glittered on the top of the shiny tower.

"This is the comet crystal," proclaimed Madame Ptolemy. "A piece of the great comet itself unveiled before you, the public, for the first time."

The crowd marveled at its shiny beauty.

"There it is!"

"I can't believe it!"

"Amazing!"

"On behalf of the Ptolemy family, allow me to welcome you to the night of the comet and invite you to join me on the roof at midnight to observe the comet fly directly above us!"

The lights in the rotunda came back on. Elle fired up her turntable. The crowd began mingling. The ghouls whispered to one another about all the beautiful dresses the royals were wearing.

Madame Ptolemy left the podium and cornered Ramses behind a pillar. "I assume this will be a traditional betrothal between my son and your daughter."

Ramses smiled nervously. "Absolutely, Madame Ptolemy. Your Ptolemy-ness. Ma'am." He dabbed his forehead with a loose bandage and slipped away to find Nefera. He caught her eyes from across the rotunda. She nodded at him reassuringly.

The ghouls were chatting in a corner about Cleo. They couldn't believe Deuce had broken up with her.

"He broke up with her for no reason?" questioned Clawdeen. "That doesn't make any sense."

"Right?" Draculaura agreed. "They were like Romeo and Ghouliet or that pea and that other pea that were in a pod together."

Cleo was off by herself, studying the comet crystal up close.

Frankie was watching her fiend closely from across the room. "Something doesn't seem right," she agreed.

Nefera approached her sister and led her over to the edge of the balcony to look down at all the guests. "Oh. My. Ra. You must be so sick and tired of hearing about Seth tonight," she said to Cleo.

"Seth Ptolemy?" Cleo was confused. No one had said anything to her.

Nefera pretended to be surprised. "You seriously haven't heard? *Everybody*'s talking about it. But if you haven't heard, I wouldn't worry about it."

"What?" Cleo was curious despite herself.

"Oh, it's nothing," said Nefera, acting like she was about to walk away. "Pretty silly actually."

"Nefera!" Cleo grabbed her by the arm.

Nefera grinned. She had her sister right where she wanted her. "Far be it from me to go fluttering around like a scarab spreading gossip, but everyone wants you and Seth to perform a Promise Ceremony under the comet tonight."

Cleo took a sharp inhale of breath. "A Promise Ceremony? Me and Seth?"

Nefera acted disinterested. "See, I told you it was silly. They are all wrapped up in the idea of the De Niles and the Ptolemys joining their families and creating the most powerful super dynasty, like ever. You've got to admit, that would be historic."

Cleo bit her lip, thinking.

"You'd be rich," Nefera said softly. "You'd be powerful. And it's what everybody wants."

Cleo gazed at the Egyptian dignitaries, at her family, at her friends. Was this really what was best? "Everybody wants me to do this?"

Nefera laughed. "Crazy, right? It would never happen. I mean you've already got Deuce..." Nefera paused, noticing Cleo's eyes welling up with tears again. "Anyway, forget I said anything."

Frankie saw Cleo looking over toward them, but she couldn't get her attention. A waiter approached the ghouls carrying a tray of snacks.

"Can I interest you ladies in some gore d'oeuvres?" she asked.

"Luna?" Operetta recognized the moth at once.

"Hey, ghouls!" said Luna. "I'm working the party. I know, it's not really acting, but, hey, I get to wear a neat costume."

Frankie was impressed. "You made it from a slice of pizza on the streets to the fanciest gala in all of Boo York. At this rate, you're going to find yourself singing on Bloodway in no time."

Luna smiled. "Ooh, try the King Tutankrab rolls. They are to die for."

Operetta hushed the ghouls. Elle was up at the podium!

"Okay, mummies and gentlemen," the DJ called out. "Make sure those bandages are wrapped up good and tight because Elle Eedee is here to make you move!" She started dancing like a robot and laughed. "It's literally the only dance I can do!"

Behind her, the comet crystal on its obelisk started to pulse with rhythmic light. Elle stared at it, mesmerized, drifting into a trance again. She buzzed and pulsed and instead of music, the room was filled with ear-splitting feedback.

"It's happening again!" said Frankie.

The ghouls pushed their way through a sea of people and made their way up to the balcony. They took Elle by the shoulders and guided her out of the party.

What was happening to her?

And what did it have to do with the comet?

Back at Monster High, Abbey and Ghoulia studied the screen. Nothing was working. The comet was still going to crash into Boo York at midnight!

# CHAPTER 17

## It's a Wrap

Cleo stared at the comet crystal in the museum. Nefera's words echoed in her head. "It's what *everybody* wants." Cleo imagined herself in front of the pyramids, holding hands with Seth, a huge crowd cheering. The ancient Egyptians would be so happy. But then a picture of Deuce, smiling, floated into her mind. He was wearing the gold beard she had given him. He took it off and flung it to the ground, where it melted instantly.

What should she do?

Cleo took a deep breath. "I am Cleo de Nile. And I've got to give the people what they want. She picked up the train of her gown and marched through the crowd to find Nefera. "I'll do it," she told her sister. "I'll promise to join our families in the Promise Ceremony with Seth." Her heart was broken and she felt cold and empty inside, but Cleo knew that she was doing the right thing.

Across the rotunda, Catty was lost in her own daydreams. She was remembering her magical time with Pharaoh. She kept finding herself humming the love song she had written with him at the top of the statue. Would she ever see him again? She had to.

Luna came over to the ghouls. "That's the end of my shift," she told them. "I've gotta fly." Her wings fluttered.

"You can't go!" exclaimed Draculaura. "Stay awhile."

Luna looked down at her waiter's uniform. "I'll have to change first."

"You better hurry," said Clawdeen. "You don't want to miss..."

But before Clawdeen could finish what she was saying, Luna had transformed. She spread her wings and circled them around herself, creating a kind of cocoon. In an instant, it cracked open and there was

Luna, wearing a beautiful gala ball gown!

Clawdeen's mouth dropped open. "Can you teach me how to do that?"

Madame Ptolemy was speaking again. "Attention, please! It is with great pleasure that I present the future of the Ptolemy–De Nile dynasty!" Holding hands, Seth and Cleo stepped forward to murmurs of interest from the partygoers. "Under the light of the great comet, my son, Seth, and Ramses de Nile's daughter Nefera…"

Ramses tapped Madame Ptolemy on the shoulder and whispered to her.

She smiled at the crowd. "I'm sorry, there has been a change. Cleo de Nile will be joined with Seth for all eternity in Boo York City's very first Promise Ceremony!"

Cleo bit her lips and held back her tears. She could see that her ghoulfriends were shocked. Behind his gold mask, Seth's eyes were darting back and forth as if he were looking for something.

Madame Ptolemy smiled. "Let me be the first to congratulate the happy couple!"

"No!" proclaimed Seth suddenly, startling everyone.

Madame Ptolemy spun around, dumbfounded. Nefera's mouth fell open. Ramses looked panicked, and Cleo looked stunned but relieved.

Madame Ptolemy glared at her son. "What do you mean, NO, boy?"

"I'm not going to do it," said Seth, determined. "I'm not going to let you take my voice away."

Something about the way he spoke caught Catty's attention. The very next moment, Seth ripped off his golden mask and behind it was the face of Pharaoh. *Seth was Pharaoh*!

He grabbed the microphone from his startled mother. "You've offered me fame and money and you want to make me the king of the world, but I'm giving it all up…"

Catty's eyes were wide with shock, and her heart was thumping in her chest.

"I have found my voice!" Pharaoh told the crowd to startled gasps and whispers. "You are not going to take it from me. I don't want to be Seth Ptolemy. I'm Pharaoh!"

He slid down the polished banister from the balcony, rapping to the crowd as he descended. His mother wasn't going to hold him back anymore. He wasn't going to hide behind a mask anymore. He wasn't going to be the king of the world—because he already was the king of the streets!

Elle whipped out her turntables and added a mix of old-school record scratching and boppin' electronic sounds to accompany him. She loved Pharaoh; everybody did! And his music was better than ever now that he didn't have to hide anymore, now that he could be who he really was and speak the music in his heart. He'd been quiet for too long!

Pharaoh had made his way through the crowd to Catty. He held out his hand to her. "*I've got you to thank*," he sang.

They began singing together, their voices weaving in and out with power and beauty, a duet nobody could resist. Everyone in the crowd was dancing and waving their arms in tune to the music—except for Madame Ptolemy.

"*Ain't nobody stopping this Pharaoh's on top of this coming back to life straight out of the sarcophagus. I'm rapping these lyrics and this corner's my scene, Boo York is my town and I'm living my dream*," rapped Pharaoh. "Can I get a boo yeah?"

Catty grinned. "Boo yeah!"

"Can I got a scare yeah?" asked Pharaoh.

"Scare yeah!" Catty responded.

"*All of you should stand up and dance no sitting, straight up out the tomb big dreams on my mind, gotta find my way in this Boo York way life!*" he sang.

"*Other towns are terrific, but let's be specific, Boo York is the best*," Catty joined in.

"*Just read the hieroglyphics!*" added Pharaoh.

"Go, Pharaoh, go, Pharaoh, go!" chanted the crowd.

Catty and Pharaoh were dancing and singing together. They were telling the world that they had found each other and that they had found a love worth singing about.

"*You're the cat's meow*," Pharaoh serenaded her. "*You're the coolest ghoul around, and your sound makes me wanna unearth myself, come from the underground.*"

"*And the time is right now!*"

"*Found each other in the Boo, now let's do it together now. Yeah!*" They finished on a high note together.

Seth took Catty by the arm and led her out of the rotunda into the dark hallways of the museum. The crowd cheered.

Up in the balcony, Nefera was fuming, her fists clenched in fury. "I don't understand! What does he have with Catty What's-Her-Face that he doesn't have with Cleo?" she said to a skeleton mummy in a top hat.

"Looks to me like it's their music," answered Toralei.

"No!" exclaimed Nefera "It's not boo-tiful; it's disgusting." She spun around, determined to solve this glitch in her plans to take over the world. "It was all going so well," she muttered to herself. "I knew persuading Cleo to do the Promise Ceremony was going to be tricky, but I never dreamed that Seth would be a problem." She stomped through the crowd in her high-heeled sandals. "But now he has to go and ruin *my* dynasty over some sick musical crush on a pop singer? *Finding my voice*? Ugh! More like, *losing my lunch*. I have to do something fast."

Nefera stopped right in front of the comet crystal. She looked up at it, thinking. "If it's music that brought those two together, then somebody needs to take it away from them." Her mind was turning over possibilities. "Whatever is spoken in the presence of the comet will be for all time," she realized.

She laughed and grabbed the comet crystal from the podium. What was she up to now?

The comet crystal was hers—and she had a promise for all of eternity she wanted to make. Now all she had to do was find Pharaoh and Catty.

# CHAPTER 18

## Promise Power Backfire

Up on the rooftop of the museum, Catty and Pharaoh were looking up at the sky, their faces aglow from the light of the comet. The roof was decorated for the ceremony with banners and statues and replicas of the strange star child who had once visited the Egyptians.

"I feel so...free!" Pharaoh was ecstatic. "You gave me the confidence to take off my mask in front of everyone! Thank you, Catty."

Catty tilted her head and grinned. "No, thank *you*. You showed me your city, your music, and helped me find mine."

Pharaoh reached out and took her hand, and they

gazed into each other's eyes, their hearts full. They didn't see Nefera emerging from the shadows, the glowing comet crystal clutched in her hand. Pharaoh and Catty were singing to each other. *"The time is right now. We've found each other…"*

Nefera held the crystal up toward the sky and intoned her wish. "Comet crystal, fragment from above, hear my declaration and make it true: The musical voices of Catty and Seth will forever belong to YOU. Take away their music—and with it, their affection for each other."

The crystal gleamed with power.

Catty and Pharaoh leaned in for their first kiss, their eyes shut. But just before their lips touched, they lurched forward and each of them felt something leaving their bodies, only they didn't know what it was. They opened their eyes, confused.

"What was that?" asked Catty.

"I don't know," Pharaoh answered, looking around.

Catty opened her mouth to sing, but nothing came out. "I…I…can't sing."

Pharaoh realized the same thing at the same moment. "Me neither."

"I feel…" murmured Catty.

"I don't feel anything," said Pharaoh. He let go of Catty's hands.

Catty looked around embarrassed. It was like she was waking up from a dream. "I'm sorry. I have no music in my heart."

Madame Ptolemy appeared on the roof. "Seth, come here immediately," she ordered. She held out his gold mask.

"Yes, Mother!" he responded. "I gotta go."

Catty sighed, but she wasn't devastated. What had she been thinking? She couldn't remember.

From the shadows, the pale light of the comet crystal shone on Nefera's evil grin. Her plan was working.

# CHAPTER 19

## Mum's the Word

**B**ack at the gala, the ghouls were talking about everything that had happened.

"So let me see if I've got this right," said Draculaura. "First, Deuce breaks up with Cleo, then Cleo decides to do that Promise Ceremony with Seth, but then Seth is like all, you know, never mind, and Seth is really that rapper Pharaoh and he wants to fang out with Catty Noir." She sighed. "And now you're saying that this party is completely out of King Tutankrab rolls?"

Luna nodded. "All of these things are true."

Frankie spotted Catty returning to the party. "Catty, over here!" she called.

But Catty walked right past the ghouls, preoccupied, as if she didn't see them.

"Catty, what's the matter?" Operetta called.

"Oh," said Catty, turning around. "Hey, ghouls."

Clawdeen rushed over to her. "Catty, we had no idea you and Seth, I mean Pharaoh, had feelings for each other…"

"I guess." Catty frowned. "I mean, we did."

"Did? What do you mean?" asked Frankie.

But before Catty could answer, the gala was interrupted by another announcement. Madame Ptolemy was speaking from the podium. "I have just been assured that tonight's unfortunate outburst by my son was merely an ill-conceived attempt at…" She coughed. "Humor."

Everyone began murmuring and gossiping. Could that really have been all that it was? It sure didn't seem funny.

"But the offending party," continued Madame Ptolemy, "has apologized and assured me that the Promise Ceremony will proceed as scheduled. Isn't that right, *Seth*?" She made sure to emphasize his name.

Looking sullen and sad, Pharaoh stepped out from behind a pillar. He was clutching Cleo's hand. Cleo held her head high. Pharaoh put his golden mask back on his face. He was Seth once again.

Out in the crowd, Mouscedes saw Nefera and Toralei off in the corner, whispering to each other. She began to put the pieces together. Nefera was involved in this. She knew it.

Nefera was handing something to Toralei. "Get rid of this!" she hissed. The crystal pulsed with the rhythm of the voices trapped inside of it.

"Mrreow! It's a deal," purred Toralei.

"Eek!" squeaked Mouscedes. "It's a deal?" She had to get to the bottom of this…fast.

# CHAPTER 20

# Singing with the Satellites

The lab at Monster High was packed to capacity. Everybody was playing the satellite game. Ghoulia tried to ignore them as she studied the data on her computer screen.

Abbey was in a panic. "You try everything! What happens if you cannot reach pilot?"

Ghoulia gestured and groaned. There would be an explosion—either of the earth or of the comet. She had to figure this out. She had to. She groaned again.

Three satellites on the screen crashed into one another with an enormous explosion, and Manny bounded out of his chair, celebrating.

"Oh yeah!" he shouted, pumping his fist into the

air. "Triple satellite score! Can't stop this!"

Manny strummed on an invisible air guitar, making feedback noises. Ghoulia whirled around, irritated at first. But then it hit her. Yes! She grabbed a piece of chalk and drew five horizontal lines through her data points. It worked! How had she not seen it before? She drew a treble clef in front of the points. They weren't noise—they were musical notes!

"There's music coming from the comet?" Abbey asked, amazed.

Ghoulia groaned in response.

"What could it mean?" wondered Abbey.

Oblivious to the game playing and air-guitar silliness behind her, Ghoulia continued studying the board. It was a code—and she was going to crack it.

# CHAPTER 21

# The Cat's Out of the Bag

Unseen in the darkness, Toralei skipped across the Hauntson River Bridge, twirling the purse Nefera had given her. She yowled an off-key tune about making a splash and getting some cash. She stopped in the middle of the bridge and pulled the glowing comet crystal out of her purse. She was just about to hurl it into the churning waters below when she stopped.

"What am I doing? I have the most beautiful voice right here in the paw of my hand, and I'm gonna just throw it in the river?" She turned the crystal over in her hand. "If this thing can take somebody's musical voice, who's to say it can't give it to somebody else?"

She shook the rock. "C'mon, rock. Give me Catty's voice! Toralei wants to sing!"

She shook the crystal like a ketchup bottle. She bit it. She put it on the ground and stomped on it. "You listen here!" she told the crystal. "I promise that I will find some way to take Catty Noir's voice…"

With the magic word "promise," the crystal pulsed and glowed brighter.

Toralei continued talking, "…*FOR MYSELF!*" The words that came out of her were a high-pitched vocal flourish. She sounded like a feline vocal diva. It had worked!

Purring to herself, perfectly in tune, she pocketed the crystal and headed back. It was time to show everyone just what she could do.

Not too far away on a street corner, Deuce was pouring out his troubles to a Boo York ghost. "So, it's like I'm stuck between a rock and uh, um…uh…uh another rock!"

"Uh-huh," yawned the ghost, barely listening.

"I either break up with my ghoulfriend, and she

gets all the rich stuff she deserves," continued Deuce, "or stay together and wreck her whole life!"

"Uh-huh."

Deuce was upset. "But I love this ghoul, and she loves me."

The ghost handed Deuce a haunt dog. "Uh-huh. I always say, you're in Boo York, you just go for it. *Relish* it." He squirted some on Deuce's haunt dog.

"You're right!" agreed Deuce instantly. "Thanks for the talk. You've really given me a lot to think about tonight. Thank you."

"Sure, kid." The ghost nodded. "Now you gonna pay for that haunt dog or what?"

"I've got to talk to Cleo!" said Deuce, racing off.

# CHAPTER 22

## A Star Is Born

Catty was sitting on the steps that led up to the museum. Frankie and the ghouls were trying to figure out what was going on. "Catty," she said, "you just sang your heart out with that boy and all of a sudden it's over? You must feel awful."

"That's the thing," Catty answered, shaking her head. "I don't feel awful. I don't feel anything. And I don't think Pharaoh does, either."

"Listen, what this ghoul needs is a healthy dose of vitamin music," suggested Operetta. "Elle, how about something in the key of Catty?"

Elle started to play "Scared of Love," but Catty just sat there.

Operetta tried to coax her. "All right, now that's the part where you start singing."

Catty just stared blankly down at the red carpet. Operetta squeezed Catty's cheeks to make her mouth move. She tried singing for her. Catty opened her mouth, but nothing came out. She couldn't do it. She just couldn't. Elle switched off the music.

"She can't sing," said Operetta. "It's like a part of her is missing."

"Her voice," announced someone standing over the ghouls. Mouscedes sat down beside them. "Her musical voice, anyway. I saw Nefera give something to Toralei. Eek! I bet she has the comet crystal!"

Frankie was nodding, trying to figure it all out. "If she wanted to get rid of the crystal, their voices must somehow be trapped inside of it."

"So how do we find her?" Draculaura wondered. "She could be anywhere in Boo York!"

Luna laughed knowingly. "If she has the singing voices of two of the most talented singers ever, then I know where she is. C'mon, ghouls, it's time to head to Bloodway."

Luna followed the bright lights to the heart of the city, and Clawdeen used her wolf hearing to identify exactly where Toralei was singing. They all snuck quietly inside and slipped into the last row of seats. Toralei was onstage belting out a show tune, and she was amazing.

"Wow!" Draculaura was impressed. "She's pretty good."

"She's pretty cheating," growled Clawdeen.

Operetta was checking her phone. "The Promise Ceremony starts in less than an hour!"

Toralei was bringing down the house. "*Get ready for a standing ovation! Buy a ticket and off we go!*"

"We have to act fast," said Frankie.

All the ghouls nodded.

Luna had a plan. "I know this show like the back of my wings. I think I know how to get the crystal back."

Onstage, Toralei was singing. She had a big brassy sound that hit every high note and could plunge down the scale to the throatiest low notes. She was going to be a star—only it wasn't really her voice that was singing.

Operetta and Elle took positions onstage with a keyboard and DJ setup. Mouscedes found an electric guitar, and Frankie sat down behind a drum set. Luna flew into the spotlight. "*Scat, cat! Get offstage, hit the bricks, this is not right, you stole that voice and I'm here* to pick a cat fight! Let it go, don't you know, onstage you're a fright. Stage fright!" she sang.

"*They call you Toralei, it should be Tora-liar, the audience should run like you're yelling 'fire.'*" Luna, wearing a police officer hat and badge, magically transformed and landed on the stage right next to Toralei. She pretended to be a writing a ticket. "*Get ready for a singing violation. Get a ticket and off you go! I'm the next big stage sensation, listen up, 'cause I came to save the show! Watch me save the show!*"

The audience was clapping wildly at this unexpected spectacle. What a show! What a hit. Upstaged, Toralei was furious.

Luna enthralled the crowd. They couldn't get enough of her. She shimmered and shone. She was a star. "*For a ghoul with stolen pipes, you talk a big game. You may fool some folks, but it's pretty lame. Let it go, don't you know, the stage is not your right. See the light.*"

Luna fluttered her wings and swooped over to Toralei—and snatched the crystal out of her hands. "You're a phony! You're no Catty, so take a catwalk!"

Catty reached out her hands and took the crystal from Luna. Her voice was back. "*Nice try kitty cat, with the voice-jack,*" she sang, hitting every note. She joined Luna onstage and the other ghouls appeared behind her, all in police costumes. It was time to stop this theatrical catastrophe!

The audience applauded. This was an amazing show. Battling feline divas!

*"I've got friends looking out, they've got my back!"* Catty was at the top of her game!

Toralei, realizing she'd been caught, was trying to sneak offstage, but Luna and Catty wouldn't let her. Catty was singing like never before. Her voice was hers, and she was never going to give it up again. What power she had! The audience cheered.

*"Now you know, stealing the show is a crime, unless you do it right, all right!"* Catty laughed as the spotlight hit her. *"You can try and imitate me, copycat, but my voice is made of more than that. You can't bite my style, let's face it, you're just catnip!"*

Catty hit the final note and brought down the house. Some people in the audience recognized her. Wasn't that the famous Catty Noir? Hadn't she dropped out of the music scene? What was she doing on Bloodway?

Toralei was dumbfounded. She tried to sing, letting lose a raucous caterwauling of sound. *"You're a catty-weirdy, yeowl!"*

The audience covered their ears.

"Get off the stage!" someone shouted.

"Booo!"

Some people were even throwing rotten tomatoes!

A stagehand tried to pull her offstage with a long hook that sent her spinning. She got tangled in the ropes. She meowed.

Catty took a bow and then another bow and raced out of the theater with her ghoulfriends, triumphant. Everyone was praising Luna for her cleverness.

"Way to go, Luna!"

"That was clawesome!"

"Luna, you were so phantasmic in there," enthused Operetta. "You're gonna be the next big star on Bloodway for sure."

"You bet she is!" The vampire director had followed the ghouls outside. He put his hand on Luna's shoulder. "I want you in my next big show—*Jersey Ghouls!*"

"Not if she's starring in *my* next Bloodway hit, *The Book of Gorgon*." A werewolf director who had been in the audience had also noticed Luna.

A two-headed-monster agent pushed through the crowd surrounding Luna. "Luna, you're gonna need an agent!" said one of the heads.

"Back off," said the other. "She's my new client."

Directors, agents, and managers were pushing close to Luna.

"Over here! You're gonna be a star!"

"Can I have your autograph?"

"Star in my revival of *Bats*!"

The ghouls were thrilled for her. "Her hard work paid off," said Frankie. "It looks like Luna finally found what she was looking for."

"And we found Catty's voice," Draculaura reminded them.

Catty held up the glowing crystal. "And Pharaoh's voice, but I don't know why it's still locked inside the crystal."

Frankie thought about it. "We may not be close enough for his voice to return to him," she suggested.

"We better get this back to the museum," Catty said, "before he and Cleo finish that Promise Ceremony."

Mouscedes stepped to the curb. "I'm on it." She put two fingers in her mouth and whistled. In the blink of an eye, three cabs screeched to a halt in front of her. "Pick a cab, any cab." She laughed like a game-show hostess. The ghouls piled into the first one.

"Wait!" called a boy's voice. It was Deuce! "I'm coming with you. Because I may not be fancy rich like the prince of Boo York, but I know in my heart that Cleo and I belong together." He caught his breath as he shut the door to the cab. "Also I've been wandering around the city all day, and I have no clue where I am."

The ghouls laughed. It was good to have Deuce back. If only they could get through traffic to get back to the Museum of Unnatural History in time.

# CHAPTER 23

## Blackout Magic

The comet was closer to Boo York than ever. It was right overhead, shining like a miniature sun, and it lit up the rooftop of the museum. Madame Ptolemy was standing before a grim-faced Cleo and a blank-faced Seth. They were going through with the Promise Ceremony, but they certainly weren't feeling in love with each other.

"It won't be long now," Madame Ptolemy noted, looking upward. "Soon, the full power of the great comet's light will be upon us."

At the edge of the assembled guests, Nefera heard her iCoffin ring. A picture of Toralei, her tongue sticking out, popped on the screen. Nefera rolled her eyes. "This had better be important," she hissed. She frowned. She could hear strange sounds in the background.

"Don't get mad," said Toralei's voice. "It's really not that big a deal, but I think you should know…"

Nefera became angrier and angrier as she listened to what Toralei was saying. "They WHAT?" she screamed into the phone. Guests turned to stare at her, and Nefera plastered a sweet smile on her face. "Excuse me."

Nefera stormed off of the roof down to the empty rotunda. "Ahhhhh!" she screamed. "All I wanted was a little help manipulating my sister into marrying a prince to make me fabulously wealthy and powerful. Is that too much to ask?"

She looked around the room and grabbed one of the ancient artifacts on display. She needed some extra magic power—and one of those old museum pieces was sure to be filled with it. She snapped the artifact in half, and the entire floor of the museum began to shake. But Nefera needed something bigger. She grabbed another and broke it open. A windstorm whirled through the rotunda. Still, it wasn't as much magic as she needed. She broke more and more ancient statues and vases and obelisks. Finally, she

cracked open a tiny amulet and all the lights flickered
and died. The whole museum was dark. Energy
swelled through the building as the magic spread. The
lights all along the city streets turned off until all of
Boo York was black.

The cab the ghouls were in was stuck in traffic.
The stoplights weren't working. Cars were honking.
People were yelling. The city was at a standstill.

Catty looked out of the window, worried.

In the rotunda, Nefera clutched the amulet. She
raced back up to the roof and looked out on the
darkened city. Only the glowing light from the comet
illuminated the gala guests.

Nefera put on her happiest voice. "Come on,
why's everyone just standing around? Let's get back to
the promising—chop, chop." She slipped the amulet
behind her back.

"She's right," Madame Ptolemy agreed. "The only
light we need is the magical brightness of the great
comet. Let us resume."

Cleo grimaced and took Seth's hand.

Comet-crazy Boo Yorkers had filled the streets to look up at the sky. The ghouls jumped out of their cab and tried to push through a sea of monsters on the sidewalks.

"Excuse me!"

"Pardon me!"

"Coming through."

"It's no use," cried Draculaura. "At this rate, we're never going to make it to the museum in time."

"We have to try," Frankie urged.

Catty looked up toward the rooftops. She had a plan! "We have to travel like mummies."

"I'm willing to try anything," said Deuce, who began walking like a mummy.

"I don't think that's what Catty had in mind," said Clawdeen, shaking her head.

Catty grabbed hold of a fire escape and pulled herself up. The ghouls followed her up, up, up and then across the rooftops, down the railings of advertisements, and through the city. They arrived at a big billboard connecting two buildings, and they dashed across the top of it like it was a tightrope.

"We are movin'!" exclaimed Operetta. "We'll be back to the museum in no time."

"Nothing can stop us now," Clawdeen agreed.

Elle froze midstep. She was having another attack. She was in a trance, buzzing and pulsing and whirring, louder than ever before.

Clawdeen sighed. "When am I gonna learn not to say things like that?"

"Oh no, Elle," cried Frankie. "It's never been this bad. We have to do something."

"But we don't know anything about robots," said Draculaura.

"But I know someone who does," Frankie remembered.

# CHAPTER 24

# The Comet Chorus

Abbey had found Ghoulia a keyboard, and she was experimenting with it. She played it slowly, following the notes from the comet that she'd charted. Everyone else in the room was too busy playing the satellite "game" to notice what she was doing—except for Abbey.

"I've got to say," admitted Abbey, "for song that comes from a destructive comet, this is a happy tune."

Ghoulia threw up her hands. If only she could figure out what it meant! Her iCoffin buzzed, and Frankie's face appeared on the screen.

"Ghoulia! We need your help!" begged Frankie from Boo York. "All the lights in Boo York have gone out, and we have to save Cleo! And now our robot friend Elle is fritzing out. Is there anything you can do to help us?"

Ghoulia's laptop was scanning the sound coming over the phone. Ghoulia squinted, listening. The strange electronic noises were actually notes! Ghoulia's eyes widened.

The ghouls were holding on to Elle as she zapped and fritzed. The comet crystal in Catty's hands glowed brighter for a moment and faded. Elle shivered and shook. She seemed to be coming out of her trance.

Frankie stared at her iCoffin, confused. Abbey's face appeared. "Sorry. Ghoulia had to go. She just figured out how to save entire world from total destruction. Bye now!" The screen went black.

The ghouls stared at one another. They looked up at the comet. What did Abbey mean—save the whole world from total destruction?

Deuce was the first to speak. "Did she just say…?"

"I'm sure it's nothing," said Clawdeen, practical as always. "Let's move."

Back in the lab, Ghoulia pushed her way through the students and teachers clustered around the computer console.

"All right, Ghoulia wants a turn!" shouted Lagoona.

Ignoring everyone, Ghoulia connected the keyboard. She stretched her fingers and cracked her knuckles like a professional pianist.

Clawd reached over and hit a note. "Hey, I didn't realize you could play the game with that..."

Ghoulia slapped his hand away. She had no time to waste. She hit a key on the computer. She touched a note and began to play. She lined up the satellites and moved them in a perfect orbit around the comet.

"She's good," whispered Twyla to Robecca.

Ghoulia played music, and the comet glowed brighter and brighter, pulsing to the rhythm of the new sounds. Was it working? Abbey crossed her fingers. She hoped so.

# CHAPTER 25

## Stop, Drop, and Rock!

The ghouls and Deuce raced across rooftops toward the museum. They dashed across ladders and wooden slats that had been placed between buildings. They swung around vents and danced over trapdoors. Catty had the comet crystal in her hand, and it was pulsing and glowing like never before.

Elle could hear the music coming straight down from the comet, and she spun her turntables in time to it as she ran. Luna spread her wings and swooped between buildings. Clawdeen and Draculaura held hands and jumped onto a fire escape. They had to get to the museum before Cleo and Pharaoh made the ultimate eternal promise that could never be broken.

"Tonight is the night of the comet," intoned Madame Ptolemy, staring up at the heavens.

Nefera drummed her fingers impatiently. "Get on with it already!"

Cleo took a deep breath. "I guess it's now or never. Everybody is looking at me. I'm Cleo de Nile, and I've gotta give the people what they want. I'm sure I'm making the right decision."

Without a voice to sing with, Seth didn't know what to say.

The ghouls were getting closer and closer! Would they arrive in time to save the day?

Ghoulia too was on a mission—to save the world. She blasted the comet's song through the satellites so everyone on Earth could hear it.

Boo Yorkers looked up at the sky, not just at the comet but at the mad pack of ghouls in gala gowns, and Deuce, racing across the rooftops. What was happening? Something. They could feel it! Everything was getting brighter and brighter as the comet got closer and closer.

Madame Ptolemy raised her arms majestically. "Now is the time for you both to speak your pledge under the magic light. Do you promise to stay together and forever unite our families?"

Cleo gulped, staring at Seth.

Seth didn't say a word.

Nefera was looking more and more agitated.

Almost out of breath, the ghouls slid onto the rooftop from a huge advertisement. Deuce bounded over to Cleo, who was just opening her mouth to seal the deal.

"Cleo! No!" begged Deuce.

Cleo was confused.

"What is the meaning of this?" Madame Ptolemy demanded.

"Cleo, don't do it!" begged Deuce. Cleo's eyes lit up, and Deuce picked her up in his arms and spun her around.

Ramses rubbed his forehead in frustration. "Oh goodie…"

Catty held the crystal up over her head. "Come, crystal, return Seth his voice NOW!"

Pharaoh shuddered as his voice shot out of the crystal and returned to his heart. He ripped off his mask and flung it in the air.

"No!" screeched Nefera. "NO. NO. NO!"

Pharaoh reached out his hands to Catty and together they began singing. Their voices were back; their hearts were open again—and it was electric.

It was as if the whole city could feel it, and lights everywhere began blinking back on.

People on the rooftop were singing with Pharaoh and Catty. Their voices filled the city. Skelicopters hovered overhead, capturing the celebration for the news. The gigantic screens in Times Scare lit up with projections of Catty and Pharaoh singing. Everyone was joining in now! It was true what they said about Boo York after all—you could find what you were looking for. Catty and Pharaoh had found their voices, and they had found each other.

Catty and Pharaoh finished their song on the same note, and all the gala guests leaped to their feet cheering. A skeleton mummy clapped so hard his hand fell off.

But Madame Ptolemy was furious. "You could have had everything. You could have created a dynasty. And this is what you want to do with your voice instead?"

With Catty's hand in his, Pharaoh was at last ready to stand up to his mother. "It's what makes me happy. This is who I am."

Madame Ptolemy looked at her son. She had never seen him so happy. She looked around at the guests all beaming. She could hear the singing and celebrating wafting up from the streets. How could she resist it? Maybe she was wrong. She gave Pharaoh a great big hug.

Cleo gazed into Deuce's eyes. "You came back," she whispered.

"I didn't want to lose you," he replied. "I'm sorry about what I said before."

"I just want the best for you—and I've got the best," Cleo said. She threw her arms around him.

Deuce blushed. "Sorry about that golden beard thingy. I didn't mean..."

Cleo pinched his chin playfully. "Forget about it. I like you better this way."

Cleo took off Deuce's sunglasses to snap a photo of him, but his gorgon eyes zapped a vulture waiter across the roof. Zap! He turned to stone and fell over.

Deuce shook his head. He was always doing that! "Sorry," he apologized.

Cleo snapped a selfie of the two of them. They were a couple again, and she wanted everyone to know! The only two monsters on the whole rooftop who weren't happy were Nefera and her father. They huddled together fuming.

"Stop all of this right now. This is not how tonight was supposed to go. This was my night. What about my power?" whined Nefera.

"What about my dynasty? This is literally the worst thing to ever happen to me!" Ramses complained.

Draculaura pointed up at the sky. "Look!" she cried. "The comet. It's coming right for us!"

No one had noticed it plummeting through the atmosphere right for Boo York. It was going to crash into the city in a fiery blaze. There was no escaping it. It was too late!

"Okay." Nefera gulped, cowering. "So maybe that is the worst thing that could happen to me!"

Everybody on the rooftop began to scream.

# CHAPTER 26

## Dance and Sing Like an Egyptian

Ghoulia was concentrating as hard as she could. She swarmed satellites around the comet. She blasted the music. All around her were students—none of whom, except for Abbey, knew that she wasn't playing a video game. She was trying to save Boo York.

"Ahh, I can't watch!" cried Manny. The tension was so high. He pulled his shirt over his eyes. He didn't want to see what happened next.

On the rooftop of the museum, everyone panicked. Monsters were crying and screaming. Mummies were running this way and that, bumping into skeletons. The ghouls didn't know what to do.

Only Catty was listening—to the music she could hear coming from the satellites, thanks to Ghoulia.

It was a beautiful melody, and Catty couldn't resist it. She began singing along. Hearing her voice, Pharaoh took her hand in his and began to harmonize with her. Guests stopped and stared at them. Draculaura and Clawdeen joined them. Then Deuce and Cleo lifted up their voices. The mummies began to sing, the dignitaries, and even Ramses and Madame Ptolemy. There was something about the song. No one could resist it. More and more people joined in all over Boo York. The chorus of their voices became louder and louder, mingling with the instrumentation from the satellites.

What no one knew was that the music had awakened the being inside of the comet. She was at the controls at last!

The comet pulsed and flared. It was right overhead. It was seconds from crashing right into the museum. Just before it hit, there was a giant flash, and the great comet exploded into a million dots of light, illuminating the entire city.

Back at Monster High, no one was sure what exactly had happened. For a few moments, no one said anything and then everyone began to cheer.

"High score!"

"Ghoulia beat the game!"

"You won!"

Exhausted, Ghoulia leaned back in her chair. Somehow she had kept the comet from slamming into the city. But why had it exploded? She didn't really know.

Little shimmering dots of light swirled among the buildings of Boo York. As the light from the comet faded away, a tiny orb hovered above the museum. What was it?

"I hear something!" said Elle. Something inside of the orb seemed to be playing the notes of the satellites. Elle played them back. A panel appeared and opened underneath the orb. A tiny star creature appeared in a beam of light.

"Ooh!" gasped the crowd.

"Aah!" exclaimed the ghouls.

"It's true! The comet came from the beings above," Madame Ptolemy cried.

"I believe this belongs to you." Catty stepped forward and handed the star being the crystal.

The beautiful star being bowed with appreciation. "Thank you. My name is Astranova. That song you heard was a distress signal—you all saved me!"

Catty, who knew what it was like to lose your voice and find it again, ran over to Astranova to give her a warm hug of welcome. "It's funny," she said, "but in a way, you were the one that saved us, Astranova. We were all searching for something this weekend, and if your comet hadn't brought us all here, or given us your song, we wouldn't have found what we were looking for."

Elle agreed. "I found the voice that was hidden deep inside of me."

"I found my voice singing loud on a Bloodway stage," said Luna.

Mouscedes beamed. "I found some amazing new ghoulfriends."

"And we found what we've always known," Cleo announced, hugging Deuce. "We're Cleo and Deuce."

"And nothing changes that," said Deuce.

Catty had never been happier. "Thank you,

Astranova, for helping everybody find their music. I know I found mine!" She gazed at Pharaoh.

Everyone crowded around Astranova, eager to get to know her.

"Your voice is so beautiful!" said Luna.

"I like your sphere ship thing," Draculaura giggled.

"Welcome! Welcome!" said everyone.

Wide-eyed, Astranova looked around the rooftop. "Are you having a party?"

"Well, it's midnight," said Cleo. "I'm in Boo York with my Deuce and my ghoulfriends. You better believe we're having a party!"

Elle started spinning discs, Catty started singing, Pharaoh was rapping, and Astranova was pulsing with light in time to the music. The whole crowd began to dance.

"I love parties!" exclaimed Astranova. She began to sing in her lovely, ethereal voice. "*We all are shooting stars. I am the light in the dark!*"

The music was magic, really magic, and everyone began rising, weightless, into the air. Luna fluttered around the party happily, playing with star particles. Astranova caught one and blew it into the crowd like a kiss.

Cleo and Deuce leaned close, touching foreheads.

"*Look up into the night. I'm falling out of the sky, falling out of the sky,*" sang Astranova.

Madame Ptolemy came up behind Pharaoh and Catty, embracing them both. She finally realized how important her son's happiness was to her.

Elle was spinning music on her turntables.

"*Be who you are! We are shooting stars! Be who you are!*"

Ramses was skulking in the shadows, disappointed, until Madame Ptolemy grabbed him and pulled him onto the dance floor.

Pharaoh was rapping. "*It's time that we rise up. It's time that we get down.*"

Catty joined in. "*Hear the sound of the whole crowd. Make the declaration out loud.*

"*It's a celebration of who we are.*"

Under the stars, the couples danced and twirled and sang. Their voices in perfect harmony, they sang a song of celebration and joy. They were lighting up the night!

"*We're shooting stars,*" sang Astranova. "*We're shooting stars.*"

The music poured out of the computer speakers in the lab at Monster High, and everyone started singing and cheering there too. Fireworks lit up the sky above

Boo York, and the heavens themselves seemed to be celebrating as beautiful colored lights glowed and pulsed across the horizon.

*"Be who you are! You are a star!"*

Cleo and Deuce were back together. Catty and Pharaoh had found their voices. All the ghouls and monsters and mummies were dancing together. Astranova too joined the dancing. At last, with a beautiful flourish, she hit a piercingly high note and everyone cheered. She was going to be a great addition to the chorus at Monster High!

# CHAPTER 27

# Star Struck

No one loved the new ghoul in school more than Operetta. She loved trying out new instruments on Astranova.

One afternoon when everyone was back at Monster High, Operetta pulled out a banjo and began playing it, her fingers flying over the strings.

Astranova raised an eyebrow and accepted the challenge. She opened her mouth to produce the exact same notes—with an extra trill and riff.

Operetta grinned and added a few extra chords. Astranova echoed them, her body shining and pulsing while the music came out of her.

Operetta plucked the strings faster and faster.

Astranova flew through the tune at lightning speed. Clapping erupted around them. Catty, Frankie, and the whole gang loved it when Operetta and Astranova decided to duel.

"Yeah, Astranova!"

"Go, Operetta!"

Operetta hopped on top of her desk, carried away with the music. Astranova hopped on top of her desk too, her notes climbing higher and higher.

Mr. Rotter was standing in the doorway. Operetta and Astranova stopped midnote.

Mr. Rotter cleared his throat. "I admire your appreciation for the musical arts, but I need to teach a lesson."

Apologetically, the girls stepped down and took their seats. But when Mr. Rotter turned to the blackboard, Operetta fist-bumped Astranova and the ghouls grinned at each other.

The music at Monster High had never been better.

On the way to her next class, Astranova heard her iCoffin begin to ring. Oops! It had been forever since she called home. "Oh, hi!" she said, answering the phone. "Sorry I didn't return your call. Traveling. But you'll never believe where I am!"

Astranova looked up and down the hallways of

Monster High. It was still hard to believe she was really here. Her phone was on videochat and she held it up so her caller could see everything. "Monster High!" she announced. "It's real!"

On the other end, Apple White, daughter of Snow White, gasped. "Ooh! Fableous!"

"Yeah and it gets better," Astranova exclaimed. "All the lands, all the high schools, that we thought were just stories? They are real! Real!"

Raven Queen crowded into the screen with Apple White. "So it IS true!"

Astranova winked and smiled. The adventure was about to begin.

# ALL-NEW
# MONSTERRIFIC MUSICAL!

NOT RATED

BRING HOME THESE
OTHER GHOULISH
MONSTER HIGH™ MOVIES!

NOT RATED          NOT RATED